UPHEAVAL

FAULT LINES
BOOK 1

HARLEY TATE

Andy blew across the surface of his coffee and risked a tentative sip before propping his feet on the edge of the closest desk. As soon as his heel hit the dented metal, pens scattered, rolling this way and that across the surface.

Sammie groaned beside him. "Can you *not* do that, Andy?" She reached out and shoved his feet to the floor. They landed with a thud. "I like to keep these in order."

He hid a smile. Berkeley Seismology Lab might be one of the premier earthquake research institutions on the planet, but post-docs tended to act like children when stuck together for hours on end. He enjoyed giving Sammie a hard time occasionally. She was always too serious, too straight-laced. He rolled toward his own desk and used the back of his chair to crack his spine.

She shuddered. "Did I miss the memo? Is it annoy-your-fellow-researcher day?"

Andy feigned innocence. "What?"

"Your back trying out to be the next Rice Krispies mascot. It's gross."

His laughter floated through the lab. "You're a scientist. Nothing should gross you out."

"I'm a landslide scientist. Not an anatomy one," Sammie shoved her glasses up her nose and scooted closer to her desk. "Don't you have some data to analyze?"

Mark poked his head out from behind the square of his computer screen. "Can you guys keep the bickering to a minimum? It's too early and I'm only on my first cup of coffee. You're worse than siblings."

"Can't make promises." Andy raised a coffee mug in his direction. "But I'll do my best."

Mark rolled his eyes before disappearing once again. Pinging around the grant-wheel roulette like a pill losing momentum, Mark had failed to land a lead investigator job in the years post-Ph.D. Being the oldest, and arguably most experienced researcher in the lab, he'd charitably been given senior researcher status. But it was a title without meaning. If the next round of grants failed to materialize, Mark might end up an adjunct professor at some community college up the coast.

They all might, eventually. Academic scientific research wasn't a field rich in opportunity or glamor, but it mattered a heck of a lot more than most people realized.

Andy brought his mug up, brain still churning over the plight of post-docs these days, and slurped. Scalding liquid sloshed against the back of his throat. He spluttered out a curse. A stream of coffee dribbled down his chin and he boomeranged forward before it stained his only white dress shirt.

As he glanced up, his gaze fell on the lower right corner of his computer screen where a constant feed from seismologic readings across the country updated every fifteen minutes. "What the..." His seat snapped upright as he rolled closer, the burn forming across his throat and tongue forgotten.

Sammie perked up. "What is it?"

Andy glanced from her to Mark's desk behind them. "Did you guys notice anything from the Pacific Northwest monitors this morning?"

"Nope." Sammie shook her head. "What are you seeing?" She pushed away from her desk and joined him, hovering behind Andy as he clicked to enlarge the open window. A section of black hair slipped over her shoulder as she leaned closer. "Well, that's new."

"What's going on?" The wheels of Mark's chair squeaked as it rolled, now empty, behind him. His shadow loomed a second later.

Sammie pointed at the screen. "It's coming from the Cascadia Subduction Zone."

Stretching from the top of Northern Vancouver Island all the way to Cape Mendocino in California, the Cascadia Subduction Zone was one of the quietest convergent plate boundaries on the planet. Unlike other subduction zones, Cascadia maintained relatively low seismic activity. Any abnormal readings were cause for alarm.

Mark jabbed his thick, black-rimmed glasses further up the bridge of his nose. "Isn't this just a tremor? They happen along the entire length every year and a half or so."

"This is way bigger than a tremor." Andy pulled up another screen. "Seismic activity is running the length of the fault at levels much higher than normal." He swallowed and the back of his throat stung. "The readings are more consistent with the lead-up to a megathrust."

"That can't be possible." Sammie shook her head in disbelief. "There hasn't been a megathrust quake on that fault since 1700."

"Researchers out of Oregon theorize there have been forty-one Cascadia megathrust quakes in the past ten thousand years." Mark's eyes never blinked, but his voice warbled on the last word.

Sammie did the math. "That's one every 243 years."

"Exactly." Panic accentuated each syllable. "The whole area is overdue."

Andy stared at the readings and poured over what he knew about the zone. Since they were in the Bay Area, the San Andreas fault received the most attention from the lab, but that didn't mean they ignored other areas of activity like Cascadia and the New Madrid Seismic Zone in the Southeast.

All over the world, megathrust earthquakes occur at convergent tectonic plate boundaries. At the Cascadia Subduction Zone, the oceanic plate Juan de Fuca slides, or subducts, below the North American plate, creating a massive fault. Over time, sediment and debris build along the fault. The resulting increase in friction locks the plates together, creating tremendous force and strain. Eventually, the fault ruptures, causing a massive earthquake as it displaces the rock above the fault upwards relative to the rock below it.

It was a cycle, bound to repeat, forever. But no one knew how to predict the next one more than a few minutes in advance. It was part of the research the lab had been involved in for years, but Andy didn't specialize in megathrusts themselves, only the aftereffects. *Tsunamis*. Monster quakes were more Mark's area of expertise.

"If it's a magnitude 9.0 or greater..." Sammie trailed off.

"The coasts of Washington, Oregon, and a good portion of California will be affected." Mark rubbed the stubble across his chin. "We're talking millions of people."

Andy leaned back in his chair, thinking over the implications. "If it's a 9.0, that's what, four minutes of continuous tremors? The resulting tsunami will flood Seattle and Portland."

"That's what happened three hundred years ago." Sammie wrapped an arm around her middle. "A dendrochronologist recently found a forest buried under Lake Washington. He theorized the entire coastline of Washington state fell into the ocean after a megathrust ruptured the fault and a tsunami hit the coast. It was one of the biggest landslides ever discovered."

"The land plummeted up to two meters, didn't it?" Mark asked.

Sammie nodded. "The topography of the coastline was radically changed. An entire Native American tribe was killed, their lands swallowed up by the ocean and turned to mud. Other tribes passed down oral history of the incident and told French fur traders in the early 1700s about it. It's how researchers knew to look for physical evidence."

A sour sensation swirled in Andy's stomach. He remembered a detail from his tsunami research. "If that's the same quake I'm thinking of, wasn't the tsunami so large it swept across the ocean and caused destruction along the Pacific coast of Japan? If I remember right, the wave was 600 miles long. The Japanese called it an orphan tsunami because they felt no earthquake before it."

"I wouldn't be surprised." Mark crossed his arms and stared at the screen. "If this isn't merely increased background activity... If this thing actually ruptures..." He trailed off, but he didn't need to finish. Both Andy and Sammie already knew what the end of his sentence would be. An earthquake of this magnitude would be apocalyptic.

"Look at the fault motion readings in the Salish Sea." Sammie pointed again to the center of the screen. "They can't be right."

"The software has never failed us before."

Sammie ran her tongue over her lips, eyes locked on the horrifying data displayed in front of them.

Mark glanced first at Sammie, then Andy. "We have to warn people. It's still showing an estimated magnitude range as high as nine."

"It makes my head spin," Sammie whispered.

"Catastrophic." Andy barely recognized the scratchy voice as his own. Gone were thoughts about permanent research positions, Mark's tenuous status in the lab, even the puckered skin lining the back of his throat. The United States was about to experience the worst natural disaster in its history.

"There's no mass early warning system in the Pacific Northwest." Mark jogged back to his desk. "Emergency alerts won't deploy until it's too late."

"What are you doing?" Sweat slicked Andy's palm and the coffee mug almost slipped from his hand as he set it down.

Mark plucked his phone off his desk and began punching numbers into the pad. "I'm getting on the phone to the lead researcher for the M9 Project at the University of Washington. He might not have seen it yet." Perspiration dotted his forehead in a glossy glitter.

The M9 Project was a consortium of researchers across disciplines who studied the Cascadia zone exclusively, focused on reducing catastrophic potential effects of a megathrust quake. Best positioned to reach news media quickly, Andy supposed. With any luck they were already on it—three steps ahead of Mark, blasting the airwaves with warning.

"Hello?" Mark's voice jittered as the call connected. "This is Mark Jamison from the Berkeley Seismology

Lab." He paused, his eyes reaching Andy and Sammie's. "Have you seen any abnormal readings coming out of Cascadia?"

He waited. "No, it's not that. Look—" He wiped a hand across his forehead. "Our data is preliminary, but the readings... They're consistent with precursor seismic activity of a megathrust quake—up to magnitude 9.0— occurring along the fault."

He paused again as a tinny voice echoed across the line. "That's what I was afraid of."

Andy's stomach churned.

Mark spoke again. "Imminent. Seattle, Portland and frankly the entire Pacific Northwest is at severe risk. I can't predict when, but the activity is off the charts. Usually, these small cluster quakes... I know you're aware, but most people won't even notice them. By the time they do, it might be too late."

The person on the other line spoke again and Mark shook his head. "We could have ten minutes. We could have an hour. Our forecasting doesn't give a timeline. All I know is, it's coming."

Andy stared at the computer screen as Mark continued to speak with someone at the M9 Project, debating the veracity of the data and what it meant. If the current readings were the lead up to a megathrust quake, then a huge chunk of the United States was about to experience something unimaginable.

He calculated the timing. A 9.0 magnitude earthquake would shake the ground for an unimaginable four minutes. Followed by a thirty-to-forty-minute reprieve wherein the ocean would be sucked away from the shore, exposing up to a mile of sand and marine life. That huge swell of water would then rebound, creating a tsunami so large, the wave would crush Seattle, Portland, and a hundred little communities in between.

Buildings not toppled in the quake would flood, homes not shaken apart would be swept inland, thousands of people who thought the worst was over would find themselves in a flash flood of epic proportions.

And as of now, no one knew it was coming.

"What about a first aid kit?" Hampton asked.

"Got it," Mika chimed in a proud voice, waving the zippered red pouch in front of the phone.

Both of Hampton's eyebrows shot up on the screen. "Wow. I'm impressed."

"Why?" Mika snorted out a laugh as she shook her head at her best friend. "Don't look so shocked. I have a whole list of items to pack. The key to packing for a trip like this is to bring the necessities only. You don't want to run out of steam two miles into a four-mile hike because your pack is too heavy."

"You can probably carry a million pounds. You've been backpacking since you were three."

"With all the plyometrics you do for volleyball, you've got this, Hampton. As long as you don't bring the kitchen sink, you're fine."

"Jumping and hiking are *not* the same thing."

Mika switched the camera view on her phone and

panned her bed. "Here, just take a look at what I'm bringing." The first aid kit was accompanied by a few bandanas, a head lamp, spare batteries, a solar charger, some emergency snacks, and a water bottle.

Hampton leaned closer, auburn curls falling across her camera. "I don't see any skittles. The whole list is suspect."

"You're lucky I can't poke you through the phone." Mika plopped down on her bed and her hairbrush slid off the comforter, clanging onto the wood floor. She groaned as she reached to retrieve it and the toe of her unpacked hiking boots dug into her side. Although she'd already packed most of her gear, she couldn't shake the feeling she'd forgotten something.

"You're lucky I haven't come down with the instamatic flu."

"I thought you saved that for Mrs. Winshear's biology exams."

The freckles across the bridge of Hampton's nose smushed together as she scrunched up her face to keep from laughing. Mika snorted and, in a moment, both girls were laughing so hard, tears leaked from the corners of their eyes. Having a friend—a real one, not one of those girls who hung out after school but ignored you in the hall—was something Mika never took for granted.

She wiped her face and propped her phone against a pillow before winding her long, unruly mane into a messy bun on top of her head. "It's going to be fun; I promise."

Hampton gave her a look. "I could think of better ways to spend a three-day weekend off from school."

"You might be dreading it now but trust me. You'll have a blast once you get there." Hampton lacked experience with the great outdoors, but they lived in one of the most beautiful places in the world with a national park basically in their backyard. Once the troop reached the first scenic overlook, Hampton would understand why Mika loved backpacking. She was sure of it.

She brought the phone closer to her face and beamed a cheesy smile at the camera. "Besides, you have me, remember?"

"I'm sure you won't let me forget."

"We'll bond and make memories."

"Hanging out with a bunch of sweaty girls who are too into their feelings, gossiping around a campfire at night?" Hampton scowled like she smelled a rotten egg. "Those kinds of memories?"

Mika shrugged. "It won't be as bad as you're envisioning."

"You'll have a transformative experience that you'll never forget, and I'll just get poison ivy and a sprained ankle."

"Think positive, Hamp. It's going to be great." She reached down and grabbed the beat-up spiral notebook off her bed and ran her eyes down the packing list. "I've got everything on my list, but I swear there's something I've forgotten."

"It's called sanity."

Mika laughed despite Hampton's serious tone. "At

least I've got a packing list. You probably threw everything in your backpack and crossed your fingers it wouldn't explode."

"Hey! Controlled chaos works." Hampton's chin jutted out in mock defiance.

"It might work for a night in Seattle, but this is backpacking. The more organized, the better." Mika hoped her best friend had at least given a little thought to what to bring.

She'd twisted Hampton's arm to join her on this trip by promising legendary views and once-in-a-lifetime experiences. But even that had failed until Hampton's parents caught wind of it. They had moved to Port Angeles from Seattle almost a year ago and had yet to convince their only child to take advantage of the opportunities living on the Olympic Peninsula provided. Once Mika explained the details, Hampton's dad practically forced her to go.

She would rather Hampton have volunteered, but Mika was determined to make the trip a success. After showing Hampton the ropes, they would both have the time of their lives away from the hustle and bustle of school, phones, and the frantic crush of everyday life.

After shoving her concerns away, she leaned into the screen and inspected Hampton's bed. Her eyes narrowed. "Wait a minute. Is that a—Hampton, no. A curling iron? Seriously? Please tell me that's not going in your backpack."

Hampton chewed on her bottom lip. "I'm bringing a

suitcase, not a backpack, and yes, it's my curling iron. I can't live without it. My hair will look limp and fried."

"That's because you curl it too often. And you can't bring a suitcase. We're hiking to our campsite, remember?"

"Can't I just walk, instead of hike? Hiking sounds so... serious."

"What else do you have there?" Mika plucked her phone off the pillow and brought it closer to her face. "Hamp—an electric toothbrush? Come on now. This has to be a joke."

"What?" Hampton almost squealed. "You expect me to not brush my teeth? They'll get as furry as the creatures roaming out there in the shadows."

"Just bring a *regular* non-motorized toothbrush."

She pinned Mika with a withering glance. "I don't have one."

"I think I have an extra from the dentist. I'll fish it out." Mika's tone turned serious. "You really can't bring all this stuff with you. It's *camping,* not getting ready for prom."

"I believe the word you're looking for is *glamping.*"

"The Girl Scouts' motto doesn't have the word *glamping* in it," Mika teased. "Besides, how are you going to curl your hair without electricity?"

Hampton arched a brow. "The cabins won't have power outlets?"

"What cabins? We're sleeping in tents."

Hampton crossed her hands in front of her face. "No.

No way. I am not sleeping one thin nylon barrier away from a bear. Not a chance."

"If you think tents are bad, just wait until you see the pit toilet."

Hampton let out a low groan and palmed her forehead. "No, no, no. I can't do this."

A laugh bubbled up Mika's throat and despite her best efforts, it burst from her lips like a chugged-soda belch.

Hampton huffed and sank onto her mattress. "I'm glad you find my demise so hilarious. I'm screwed."

"You're not screwed, and this is nowhere near a demise. Just think of it as an adventure."

"I'm hopeless in the outdoors," Hampton pouted.

Mika waved her off. "That's because you've never spent any time in them."

"I'm afraid of bugs. They're icky. Just like my hair will be once I'm in that damp wilderness for half an hour."

"You're just a city girl. You'll adapt. You always have."

"I won't argue with that." She exchanged a knowing glance with Mika.

After an accidental collision in the hallway on the first day of school led to a frantic attempt to rinse half a Mocha Frappuccino out of Mika's sweater, the girls became instant friends. Once they shared a late-night confessional about family drama—Hampton's abrupt move from Seattle to Port Angeles and Mika's mother's

disappearance to Bellevue and separation from her dad—
they became inseparable.

Mika and her mother were trying to mend the hurt
between them, and it was getting better, but they still had
a long way to go. She'd been struggling until Hampton
came along. Even if Hampton doubted her ability to
survive a weekend in the wild, she'd overcome worse and
helped Mika do the same.

She checked the time on her bedside clock. "Shoot.
I've gotta run." She cut Hampton an apologetic glance.
"I'll see you at school?"

"I'll be there whether I want to or not," Hampton
joked.

"You better be." As she shoved her phone in her
pocket it buzzed. Mika pulled it out. A text from her dad.

*Hi sweetheart. Hope you have a good trip. Remember
the first aid kit.*

Mika smiled, punching a response into her phone's
keypad. *Thanks, Dad. I've got the kit, no worries.*

A moment later, her phone buzzed again.

I'll see you Sunday afternoon when you get home.

Sounds great, Dad. Mika tossed her phone onto her
bed, shoved the last few items into her pack, and hauled it
onto her shoulders. She grabbed an extra bottle of water
from the fridge, her keys, and headed toward the car.

She smiled as she unlocked the door. Her dad had
scrounged up the money for a used Honda hatchback when
she turned sixteen and Mika could hardly believe it. It
wasn't flashy and had a dented rear bumper, but it was

reliable, and it was hers. With her dad working the early shift at the Port and her mom living her own life in Bellevue, it was her only means of making it to school on time.

With one last glance at the house, she pulled out of their driveway. White painted wood, black shutters, faded red door. The shrubbery around the porch was a bit unruly and the grass needed a mow thanks to the early spring this year. But it was home—familiar and warm and lived in. Loved.

Mika navigated through their quiet neighborhood, heading toward her high school and the van waiting to drive her Girl Scout troop to their camping spot. In a few hours, she would be immersed in the beauty of the mountains, forgetting all about homework and grades, and her parents' separation. She couldn't wait.

CHAPTER TWO
CLINT

Clint Redshaw stood by the water cooler in the break room of the Port, typing in a last text to his daughter.

"What's that big grin on your face for?"

"Hmm?" Clint, distracted, lifted his eyes from his phone.

Jack Stevens, the head scheduler, bent over the water cooler, pushing the spigot down until his Styrofoam cup filled. The water jug glugged in protest.

Clint shoved his phone into his back pocket. "Nothing, it was just Mika texting me."

"Oh, what's she up to? Get another A on a test?"

"She just left for a Girl Scout camping trip for the weekend."

Jack propped his shoulder onto the wall, leaning into it. "Well, that sounds fun."

"Tell me about it. I wish I was with her."

"You aren't one of those helicopter parents, are you?" Jack teased, drawing the cup to his lips and slurping.

Clint frowned as he debated Jack's question. He certainly tried to give Mika space if she needed it. She'd had a rough time ever since the separation, and he wanted to make sure she felt comfortable, loved, and respected.

If she needed him, he was there in a flash. If she wanted to be left alone, he dodged her until she came around again, cheeks rosy, infectious smile lighting up Clint's entire world as she chirped about something exciting that happened in her day.

"No. Well, I try not to be." Clint shrugged as he reached for a cup. "Although she may have a different opinion on that."

"I'm sure she thinks you're a rock star dad," Jack offered with a kind smile.

Clint crossed his fingers. "Here's hoping."

He didn't want to admit that he contemplated calling in sick and letting someone else run the all-day strategic planning meeting just so he could camp and hike with his daughter. It wasn't like the team couldn't handle it without him. As the facilities manager, Clint's role was more implementation versus conceptualization, but he was still required to attend.

Jack straightened himself out from the wall and scratched his elbow. "I know what it's like. I've got Ava and Megan." He paused, smiling introspectively at the gray carpet. "I feel like there's no happy medium. They either hate me or they love me. Of course, they love me whenever they can use my credit card." He glanced up with a smile on his face, but Clint got the feeling the man sought affirmation.

He tried to relate, rolling his eyes and laughing, but the truth was, he didn't. Mika didn't have a credit card and she'd never even asked for one. It seemed like dangerous territory he wanted his sixteen-year-old to have no part of. But Mika was a good kid. She'd never given Clint a reason not to trust her.

"You and your ex ever disagree on the money thing with your kid?" Jack asked. "It's all my wife and I ever fight about. Whether the girls are spending too much, whether we spoil them, yada, yada."

Clint scratched behind his ear. Was she his ex? He pushed the thought aside. "Honestly? I try to stay out of Daphne's way and she stays out of mine. Since she moved to Bellevue..." he searched for the right words... "We don't talk unless we have to."

"Gotcha."

"Gentlemen." A woman from the City of Port Angeles's budgeting office entered the breakroom, all business in a gray skirt suit and heels. Jack raised an eyebrow at Clint and nodded in the woman's direction, but Clint waved him off. The last thing he needed was a romance with some woman who knew nothing about the Port other than line items on a spreadsheet.

Besides, he wasn't interested in anyone other than Daphne. They weren't divorced, merely separated. Sure, it had been over a year at this point, but Daphne never served him with papers. Until then, he was giving her space. She wanted to be a paralegal at some high-powered law firm in the big city. Leave her husband and kid and what, find herself?

Fine. He could hold down the fort, at least for a little while longer. With the modernization plan plowing full steam ahead, and Mika beginning to be interested in college and grades and boys, he'd been busy.

He'd always told his daughter that the world didn't stop for anyone. It was a fast-moving train, and if you wanted to be a part of it, you'd have to jump on before it left you behind. He worried about Mika, wanted her to be safe and happy despite the separation. His thoughts kept shifting back to her and the backpacking trip, a gaggle of girls out in the woods, watching the sunrise over a steaming cup of hot chocolate, learning wilderness skills he wished he could teach her.

"Earth to Clint. You in there?"

He blinked back to the present. "I'm sorry, what?"

Jack shook his head with a smile. "We were discussing the modernization. Beth asked about the log haulers."

The woman smiled one of those detached, professional smiles that meant anything from "you're full of it," to "I really need to pee."

"Sorry, I'm a bit distracted today."

"Oh?"

"My daughter's camping this weekend."

She pointed in the air like some sign hung beside her. "And that's why I never had kids. Can't stay focused on the job when you're worried about a scraped knee or a fever."

Clint hid his expression with the Styrofoam cup. "To each their own."

He followed Beth and Jack into the small conference room on the western side of the warehouse. A single, long window cut into the corrugated metal, revealing the massive semi-circle port and a large barge half-full of timber. A loading crane dangled over the barge, a load of prepped logs swaying in its grip.

The woman from the break room took up position at the head of the table and smiled at the employees as they filtered in. With only thirty full-time employees, the Port ran a lean crew. She rested her fingertips on the table and cleared her throat to begin.

"Hello everyone. For those who I haven't met, my name is Beth Transom, and I'm head of budgeting for the Port Commission. As you know, we have been working hand-in-hand with your Executive Director, Mr. Rechio, to finalize the five-year strategic plan for the Port of Port Angeles and align your goals with the community as a whole."

Clint twisted his Styrofoam cup around on the table, attempting to stay focused.

"We have established four main goals for the Port. First, to aggressively market the Port, including further development of the Marine Trades Industrial Park, leveraging the Composite Recycling Technology Center to bring research and investment dollars to Clallam County, and continue to acquire strategically located industrial property for further development."

Jason Rechio, Clint's boss, leaned forward in his

chair. "As the Port Commission has made clear, we've broadened our focus this past year away from wood-products manufacturing and into other areas. While we recognize the timber industry is the largest employer in the immediate vicinity, that doesn't mean they should be our sole focus."

"The Commission agrees. Over the next five years..."

The words drifted into the background as Clint tuned out. He thought once again of his daughter, probably halfway up the mountain by now. Something nagged at him, but he couldn't place it. He'd checked in, she'd texted back. He glanced out the window. Weather was fine. But the feeling lingered.

He wished he could always be there for Mika. And he tried. Truly. But his job ate up the hours, and he often felt tugged between two worlds. With Daphne now living in the big city, she couldn't be involved in the day-to-day. Mika had been forced to adapt and grow up over the past year and it pained Clint to admit he was partly to blame.

His turn finally came to present, and Clint stood, shoving his thoughts of his daughter down to focus on the spreadsheet in his hand. "As Jason mentioned, one of our key areas here at the Port is log barging. Our waterfront log yard is already an efficient and productive way to ship logs originating in Canada, Alaska, and areas within Puget Sound to markets in Oregon and regional lumber mills. Over the past three years, the yard has been continuously at or near capacity."

"Have you investigated other forms of barging to drive additional revenue?"

Jason spoke up. "We have, but we do not believe current market conditions support it at the moment."

Beth pressed her lips together. "You're aware one of the main goals of this strategic plan is to foster living wage jobs in the area. Bringing in non-log barging might realize this vision."

Jason nodded and spoke again, launching into a detailed debate on the merits of the proposal. Clint glanced back out the window at the Strait of Juan de Fuca. The same feeling gnawed at him, deep in his gut. Try as he might, he couldn't suppress it. Mika needed him.

He checked his watch. She should be on the road, halfway to the parking lot in the Olympic National Forest. If something happened, she would call. And he would drop everything to protect her, no matter what it might cost him in the end.

CHAPTER THREE
DAPHNE

"Come on, come on." Daphne chewed her bottom lip and coiled her fingers around her briefcase, knuckles white and patience thinning.

She rolled the window down and craned her neck out over the sea of brake lights, struggling for a better view of the traffic.

"Could you not do that? It lets in exhaust."

Daphne glanced up front and pressed the window button as she tried to keep it together. The poor rideshare driver was doing his best, but it wasn't good enough.

A car behind them blared his horn. She twisted around and tossed the driver an angry scowl. "What do you want us to do about it?" She huffed between clenched teeth. "We can't move if the people in front of us don't."

Telling the guy off did nothing to calm the nervous patter of her heart against her ribcage. Why a gridlock nightmare today of all days? The one day she couldn't afford to be late this week. Traffic in the greater Seattle metro was always problematic, something she was adapting to since leaving Port Angeles. But today it was on steroids.

Daphne dared a glance at the dashboard.

8:45 a.m.

The deposition started at 9:30 and she needed to stage the exhibits, prep the conference room, and appear in control and calm when her boss walked in. She was as good as screwed.

Stop, start. Stop, start. Pump the gas, hit the brake. At 9:10, she leaned forward and pointed out the window. My building's just up there. I'm getting out. I'll tip you extra."

The driver unlocked the car and Daphne rushed out, almost dropping her briefcase as she slammed the door shut. She ran the several hundred feet to the building, rushed through the lobby doors, and bypassed the elevator to take the stairs two at a time. Almost tripping on the last step, Daphne busted into reception of Lormack and Higgins, one of Bellevue's top boutique law firms, in a whirlwind.

"Sorry, sorry I'm late." She flapped her hands in the air, ignoring the glare from the receptionist as she hurried down the hall.

With her heart still pounding like her daughter's choice in music, she threw her bag onto the carpeted floor in her cubicle and clicked her mouse to wake the desktop computer. Sweat ran in a rivulet down the small of her back and her blouse stuck to her skin beneath her suit jacket.

Daphne worked hard to get this job, taking paralegal classes while still at home in Port Angeles, interviewing when Mika was at school. She refused to let a hiccup in rush hour traffic stand in the way of her goals. If only her boss, Don Lormack, cared an iota for his employees. As far as he was concerned, paralegals were fungible.

"Load, you stupid thing," Daphne hissed through clenched teeth, swirling the mouse on the pad. At last, her computer revved to life, and she checked her email for any last-minute exhibit changes.

She cursed.

Lormack asked for a rearrange of exhibits 1-10 for every binder. She checked the wall clock. Eight binders. Ten minutes. Her tongue stuck to the roof of her mouth like a high heel in wet concrete.

She pushed her hair off her shoulder and typed in a whirlwind, rearranging the binder table of contents as fast as her fingers would allow. After hitting print, she rushed to the copy room to find Becca, another paralegal, standing at the copy machine.

Daphne forced her voice to stay even and light. "Big job?"

Becca turned around, face paler than usual, her lanky figure all limbs as she jostled a bulky gusset, tips of papers and folders bursting out from the top. "I was just getting started. Need something?"

"Just a quick handful of copies if you don't mind."

She whisked the print out of the printer and shoved it in the copy machine before hitting the button.

Becca was young, in her early twenties. And although Daphne liked her, an undercurrent of competition ran through the office. Daphne was trying to carve her way into the firm; a woman in her forties embarking on a new career. A strange breed.

When everyone else met for drinks after work, she was often conveniently left off the email invite. She blamed it on the age gap—most of the staff had more in common with Mika than Daphne—but it stung. Still, she did her best to keep her head above water.

It was sink or swim, a far cry from Port Angeles, and she mostly thrived on it.

When she'd met Clint at the University of Washington, they were both set on living the big city life, full of late nights and long hours and the hustle and bustle of it all. But when Daphne became unexpectedly pregnant, the calculus changed. Clint landed the job at the Port and they couldn't turn it down. It paid more than double any other offer and Daphne wouldn't need to work.

No daycare. No big city. No bright lights. Just a sleepy coastal town and a chubby little baby who turned overnight into a self-reliant teenager who didn't need her. Not like she used to.

Daphne had been adrift. Unmoored and lonely. Clint had his job, Mika had school, and as she'd grown up, she'd grown closer to her father. They loved the same things—anything involving the outdoors, mostly—and Daphne had been left at home, alone.

When she stumbled upon the online paralegal course, she intended to merely learn the trade, not apply for a job. But the school offered placement assistance. After the interview at Lormack and Higgins, she found herself accepting the offer before even telling Clint or Mika what she'd done.

And now she was here, living the life she thought she always wanted. The copier finished and she shook herself back into the moment.

Becca gave Daphne a commiserative smile, her skin taut with youthfulness. "That bad, huh?"

Daphne bristled. "Traffic was rough." She nodded at the gusset. "Looks like you've got your hands full, too."

Becca's face twitched in a fleeting moment of disappointment, and she hugged the bundle closer to her chest. "Just making a working set for Mr. Higgins."

Daphne plucked the papers off the copier, punched them quickly, and waved at Becca. "Good luck."

"You, too." Becca's voice grew fainter as Daphne rushed down the hall. She set the stack of papers on her desk and grabbed the first of the binders, swapping out the table of contents and rearranging the exhibits per her boss's request.

As she grabbed the second binder, her phone dinged and a picture of her daughter laughing lit the screen. *Mika.*

Daphne swiped the screen. *Hey Mom, I'm heading to my camping trip. Just wanted to let you know.*

She treasured every moment her daughter reached out. Their relationship wasn't perfect, especially after her surprise move, but they were working on it and making progress.

Daphne typed out a response. *That's great sweetie. Did you get everything packed?*

Mika responded almost instantly. *Yup. Good to go.*

Great. I hope you have fun. Send pics.

Thanks Mom. I'll try. Might not have cell service though.

Daphne wished she could find better ways to bond with her daughter. But Mika showed little interest in visiting Bellevue or downtown Seattle. Shopping, fancy restaurants, and salons held no interest for her. She'd pick a week in the woods with her dad over the best the big city could buy every time. So Daphne swallowed the disappointment and supported her daughter. She sent her a quick heart emoji and set the phone down as footsteps sounded behind her.

"Something more important than pulling those binders together?" Don's booming voice thundered through Daphne's personal space.

She winced before turning to face the wrath.

Don stood in front of her, his salt and pepper hair slicked back and his lips pinched into a disapproving pleat.

"Sorry, it was just my daughter. She's leaving for a camping trip, and I was making sure she—"

"I don't care if your mother is dying on the operating

table. This deposition makes or breaks this case Ms. Redshaw. You know that."

Daphne swallowed and nodded diplomatically. Arguing was useless. "Understood."

Don's eyes reached the binders sprawled across Daphne's desk. "How long?"

"Just as soon as I can, Mr. Lormack." Daphne shoved her hands behind her back to hide a tremor.

"Work harder, faster, Daphne." His voice was clipped and disappointed. The space around them fell dead quiet.

Her cheeks heated with embarrassment. A grown woman getting dressed down by a man barely older than her, but what could she do?

"I would have had them put together earlier but traffic was insane." She regretted offering the excuse as soon as it left her lips.

"It doesn't matter what the reason is. Just get it done. I don't have time for this." Don's eyes flashed with impatience before he straightened his red power tie and turned his back, stomping toward the conference room.

Daphne sunk into her desk chair and went back to work, willing her hands to stop trembling. Don was such a jerk. What gave him the right to yell at her in front of everyone? At the very least he could have pulled her into his office, shut the door to give her a lecture. But no, Don, like most big-city attorneys, thrived on drama and attention.

"Don't let him get to you."

Daphne swiveled in her chair to find Andre, one of the legal assistants, offering a sympathetic smile.

Andre was Daphne's only friend in the office. He didn't mind her age, loved coffee as much as she did, and always managed to brighten her day. If he didn't work there, she wasn't sure she'd have lasted this long.

"Thanks," Daphne squeaked.

He leaned in conspiratorially. "He's just a bully. But you didn't hear that from me."

Daphne's lips curved into a smile, something only Andre could tug out of her. "Don't worry. I hear it in my own head a hundred times a day."

Andre's eyes glinted. "Do you need some help?"

"Do you have time?"

"A few minutes to spare." Andre worked for one of the other partners, a woman who wasn't nearly as hot around the collar as Lormack.

"You're a lifesaver." Daphne breathed out a sigh of relief.

"No, I just work for a human, not a robot." Andre grinned and reached for a binder.

"Still, I'd be lost without you."

"Don't you forget it."

Daphne shoved the embarrassment and guilt out of her mind and focused on the task at hand.

Mika pulled into the parking lot of her school where a white and blue van waited. A gaggle of girls milled about and a pile of packs teetered by the open door.

Hampton leaned against the van by herself, legs crossed at the ankles, absentmindedly picking at a nail as if she needed to occupy herself with something. The morning sun caught her curls and turned them almost orange in the sun.

Mika parked, pulled her pack out of the trunk, and eased it over both shoulders before heading toward her friend. She bumped her shoulder against Hampton's. "Keeping the van upright?"

Hampton sagged with relief. "Thank goodness you're here." She whispered so softly, Mika strained to hear.

"Hamp, relax." She slid her backpack off her shoulder. "You look like you're going to have a panic attack."

"I might." Hampton leaned closer. "I don't think I

should go."

"What? Why?"

"Are you guys talking about the campsite?" One of their fellow troopers, a girl named Sasha, approached with a smile. She tucked a stray strand of brown hair behind her ear. "I heard it's a four-mile hike-in." Her eyes widened in excitement. "All uphill."

No wonder Hampton's freaked. Mika pointed to the paperback in Sasha's grip. "Anything good?"

She held it up a bit sheepishly. "For the road. Thought I'd brush up on my spooky stories for the campfire tonight."

"Redshaw?" Ms. Rogers, one of the two chaperones, called out to Mika, shielding her eyes with the palm of her hand.

"I'm here," Mika confirmed.

Ms. Rogers waved her over. "Bring your things to the back so we can load up."

Mika smiled at Sasha, squinting against the sunlight. "Counselor's orders." She grabbed her bag and headed toward the van with Hampton hot on her heels.

"I was talking to Sasha earlier," she hissed, her voice crackling with worry.

Mika frowned. "Okay, so? Is that against the rules or something?"

"No, but—I don't know. She said this camping area we're going to is pretty remote."

"It's in the mountains. Of course it's remote. It's probably completely off the grid."

Hampton's face paled and she shoved her thumbnail

back beneath her teeth.

"Oh, come on, Hamp." Mika gave Hampton's arm a playful swat as she unclipped her smaller day pack from the larger backpack. "We went over this already, remember? The fact that you couldn't bring your entire supply of hair grooming products if they needed an electric plug?"

Hamp winced. "Well, my hair is going to frizz out, just warning you."

Mika patted her on the back and shoved her bag in the back of the van. "Thanks for the warning."

"You're not funny." Hampton scowled.

"Of course I am," Mika teased.

"Alright ladies." Ms. Rogers's voice cut through the swarm of girls. "Time to cover the ground rules."

A slew of groans filtered through the group.

Ms. Rogers paused to let the complaints die down before continuing her speech. She lifted a green sack and opened it. "This is for your cell phones. I want them powered off and in the bag. This is a nature trip, no distractions will be permitted."

Another round of groans, the biggest coming from Hampton.

"It's going to be fine," Mika encouraged her friend. "You'll have me to keep you company."

Hampton gave her an apprehensive glance before reluctantly powering off her phone and dropping it into the bag.

"If you haven't loaded your gear, get it stowed safely in the back and find a seat in the van. We're a full house this trip, so no empty seats. Ms. Chalmers and I will sit up front."

Mika dragged Hampton onto the van, scoring one of the two-seat clusters across from the narrow aisle. She liked the other scouts attending the trip, and would have welcomed sitting by Sasha or Madison or any of the other girls, but Hampton seemed freaked out and Mika wanted to calm her down. Being forced to make small talk with girls she didn't know—girls who were *really* into camping —might tip her over the edge.

While everyone situated themselves in the van, Ms. Chalmers counted heads. "That's everybody!" She shut the side doors and hopped up into the passenger seat as Ms. Rogers started the engine. They wound through the handful of streets between the edge of town and the high school and turned onto Hurricane Ridge Road. Almost immediately, the van began to climb.

Hardwoods, lush with early summer leaves, hugged the road with towering pines reaching toward the cobalt sky behind. As they climbed, the pines took over, branches reaching for the edges of the asphalt.

"It doesn't even look real," Hampton said, her eyes transfixed on the window.

"What doesn't?" Mika rooted through her small bag and pulled out a word search and a pen.

"The mountains."

Mika glanced at her friend, eyebrow raised. "When you said you were a city girl, you really meant it, huh?"

Hampton's eyes were wide as she nodded. "Yes. What part of that didn't you get?"

"I just figured you'd at least driven through here by now. You've been in Port Angeles for months."

Hampton shook her head. "My parents aren't the outdoorsy type, remember? As soon as they found out about this camping trip, they booked a weekend at some fancy hotel in downtown Seattle. It's dinner and shopping and visiting old haunts all weekend."

Mika pointed out the window. "I think this beats any of that, don't you?"

Hampton turned. "It's growing on me."

"See? The great outdoors isn't so bad."

A wrinkle perched itself in the center of Hampton's forehead. "Well, I don't know about *that*. Let's see if you'll still be saying that after we have a million bug bites tonight."

"That's why there's bug spray in my bag."

Hampton pinched her lips together, giving Mika a skeptical eyebrow. "You have an answer for everything, don't you?"

"And you're just now learning this?" Mika joked.

Hampton rolled her eyes. "I wish I had my headphones."

"They won't work without your phone anyway," Mika reminded her.

"Don't get me started on that."

"By the end of the night, you won't even miss it."

"Fingers crossed." Hampton's chin dipped and she studied her hands clasped in her lap.

It had been weeks since Mika had left all the stresses of teenage life behind. Homework, tests, navigating uncertain social waters, cross-country in the winter, track in the spring. She was scheduled from the minute she woke up until the minute she went to bed and no matter what she did, she always felt like she was falling behind. But a weekend out in the woods did wonders. It calmed and centered her. Made her problems seem small and easy. Hampton would feel that too, she knew it.

Mika reached over and tugged on one of Hampton's curls. "Appreciate the setting. We'll be there in no time. If we're going where I think we are, there's some long-range views near the campsite that will take your breath away."

Hampton looked uncertain but managed a smile. "I hope you're right."

"Owwww," Madison jostled in the seat in front of Mika. "Your elbow is digging into my side."

"Sorry," came a voice from the other seat.

"Alright, girls," Ms. Chalmers called out, as if on cue. "It's time to get along and have some fun." She swiped her arms through the air as if she was a conductor leading an orchestra and began to sing. The long-time scouts knew the tune well and the van erupted into an off-key chorus.

Mika bumped her knee into Hampton and smiled as she sang.

"You actually know the words?"

Mika sang louder and nodded.

Hampton craned her neck, gawking at the other girls singing along. "Wow."

"Oh, come on," Mika nudged her. "It's fun. And

everyone else is enjoying it. After the weekend you won't be able to get these songs out of your head."

Hampton scoffed. "That's a stretch."

They continued to climb the winding mountain road, the terrain growing more rugged as they left civilization behind. The van shook and Hampton stiffened. Ms. Rogers eased her foot off the gas and braked as they slid around a curvy bend.

"It's okay," Mika whispered, giving her friend a soothing smile. "It's just the elevation change. The van's loaded with gear. The engine's probably struggling to keep the speed."

Hampton licked her lips and nodded, tossing a wary glance out the window. "Are you sure? This incline is really steep. I know all we can see is trees, but there's no guard rail to protect us if we go hurtling down the mountain side."

"That's not going to happen," Mika promised. "Ms. Rogers is a great driver."

Hampton lifted shaky fingers to her forehead to blot at a few beads of perspiration dampening her hairline. She nodded, but her eyes clouded with worry.

The ascent began anew and Ms. Rogers floored the gas as they chugged up a steep hill. The van shuddered again. Hampton sucked in a sharp breath. Mika gripped her friend's hand, squeezing reassurance into it. "Maybe the tires are old. If the tread isn't grippy anymore, all this weight in the back could give the van a real challenge."

"You really think that's all it is?"

Mika glanced out the window. "I'm sure of it."

CHAPTER FIVE
CLINT

The first tremor caught Clint unaware. He scooted his chair in, assuming Jack bumped him from behind while squeezing past.

Jason paused mid-sentence, brows knitting for the briefest second before he pressed on.

Another vibration rumbled through Clint's chair and the inch of water in his Styrofoam cup rippled.

"Did anyone feel that?" Mary's voice tipped into alarm.

Clint swallowed down a lump of disbelief and stood. "All right, everyone. We all know the drill. This could be nothing or something big, but let's not take any chances. Earthquake evacuation procedures. *Now.*"

The woman from the Port Commission—Beth, he reminded himself—balked. "Seriously? I didn't feel anything."

As soon as the words left her mouth, the entire building shook. Windows rattled in their casing and the walls groaned as the metal exterior undulated. Beth's painted lips fell open and her fingers splayed across the desk surface.

"Like I said, earthquake procedures. Let's get moving." Clint clapped his hands and the entire room hopped into action. The handful of employees still sitting shoved their chairs back and hurried toward their assignments.

The lobby and any visitors belonged to Mary, the receptionist. Scott pressed his phone to his ear, already calling the on-site vendors. Veronica hurried toward the marina. Thanks to Clint, they trained quarterly on this exact evacuation procedure, with a task assigned to everyone. Clint hoped the Port employees remembered what to do. If so, it would go smoothly.

Jack hovered at the interior door. "I'll get to the lot, start waving people over."

"I'm heading to the docks. Rally point in the South lot in five." Clint strode toward the door leading directly outside.

"W-what about me?" Beth stammered. "I-I just moved here from New Jersey. We don't have earthquakes!"

Jason reached for Beth's arm. "Come with me. We'll grab your things and head to the meeting area."

Clint gave his boss a quick nod of thanks and ducked outside. He didn't have time to babysit a woman who didn't have a clue when almost thirty employees and countless contractors were working the Port. He jogged toward the busiest sector where a crane arm loaded with logs swung out across a barge.

Hands in the air, he waved down Jimmie, the forklift operator, who waited for the crane to deposit the load before digging up another stack.

Jimmie shifted into park and pulled off his ear protection. "What's up?"

"Can't you feel that?" The ground beneath Clint's feet vibrated.

"Can't feel anything over the rev of the engine."

"There's ongoing tremors!" Clint waved at the ground. "Mild for now, but who knows what's coming. Get your crew to the South lot ASAP."

"We aren't done loading."

"You know the rules. Follow the quake procedures. *Now*, Jimmie. I don't want to tell Kim you died loading logs when you should have been evacuating."

Jimmie's pale face flushed, and he nodded in agreement. "Will do."

Clint crossed the man and his three coworkers off his mental list. He hurried toward the barge. A man stood on the dock, trying to steady the temporary stairs leading to the barge deck. Clint cupped his hands around his mouth and shouted. "There's earthquake risk! You need to push off. Get out to sea!"

The man turned and shook his head. Clint was too far away to hear. He picked up the pace, jogging the last twenty feet. The dock swayed violently to the left and he stumbled. "Earthquake!" He shouted at the man. "Get your people on the barge and pull out of the port."

"Engines aren't fired up. It would take—" Another tremor stole his breath and the man fell against the steps.

Clint staggered three steps to the right, barely staying vertical. "If you can't leave, then disconnect at least. I can't guarantee the dock won't suffer damage."

The man nodded and grabbed the stair rails with both hands before hauling himself up. Clint exhaled. It wasn't ideal—a barge staying in port risked massive damage—but at least they were warned.

He turned toward the warehouse, and another jolt of the ground buckled his knees. The ground rose in his vision and he landed, palms spread, face an inch from the concrete. Violent tremors shook the dock, an order of magnitude greater than anything he'd felt before. The port-a-potty ten feet away slid in his direction. A door flew open on the shed housing dock repair equipment and a stack of buckets crashed to the ground.

Dirt clung to Clint's palms as he struggled to stand, but the tremors rocked the dock, splintering the asphalt beneath him and forcing him back down. If the shaking continued much longer, the entire structure would break apart.

Across the U-shaped concrete pier, two tractor trailers queued, full of logs ready for loading on the barge. Clint watched in horror as another wave of tremors jolted the dock. One trailer skidded sideways, logs tipping from the open back as it crashed into the guard rails.

Careening over in a slow-motion disaster, the trailer lost logs as it slid. Giant rough-cut pine trees careened across the broken concrete, dropping one at a time into the turbulent waves.

Smoke billowed from beneath the cab as the driver stood on the brakes. It was no use. The weight of the trailer dragged the cab toward the water. At the last minute, the cab door opened and a man jumped out, landing hard on the asphalt as the cab rolled off the dock and splashed into the water.

Clint sagged against the ground, relieved the man survived. But it was short lived. A giant rumble like thundering hooves of a herd of buffalo echoed behind him and he turned to see a cascade of logs rolling in his direction. The logs had been stacked in bundles, waiting for Jimmie or one of the other forklift operators to feed them to the crane.

Now they cascaded toward him, bouncing and bobbing and gaining speed. Clint struggled to his feet as the quake, still going strong, wrecked the reinforced dock and pier. The concrete and asphalt, strong enough to support countless logging trucks loaded to the brim, now crumbled beneath his feet. Every step, he sunk lower into the once solid material.

One step, then another, running and staggering, swaying three feet in one direction and four in the other, Clint managed to stay on his feet. The logs gained. He felt their insistent, unrelenting beat, above and beyond the shaking of the earth.

The guard house, usually empty, stood at the edge of the dock, half on the solid ground, half on reinforced piers. Clint dove for it, ducking behind the edge of the building as the first log clipped his heel. Giant logs careened past him, a teeming mass of forest bent on destruction. The first slammed into a little hatchback parked at the entrance to the dock and another followed, rolling up and over the first to crest the tiny car's hood.

The windshield cracked, the hood dented, and the roof caved in. The little car never stood a chance. Neither did Clint. He sucked in a lungful of air and thanked God for his good fortune. He survived.

Leaning over and gripping his thighs, he used the guard shack as support, bracing against the quake. Never in all his years living in the Pacific Northwest had a quake gone on this long. Thirty seconds? Sure. He'd heard of some lasting a minute. But what was this? Two minutes? More?

A giant crack sounded behind him and he pulled away from the shack. Massive, jagged cracks split the dock in two. Piers buckled. A forklift fell sideways and landed in a chasm, dangling a foot out of the water.

Clint hoped Jimmie and the crew listened and were safe at the rally point. It was too late for anyone stuck on the dock now. He stared out at the barge. It swayed violently in the water, escaping logs rolling across the deck. Too much more of this and he doubted it would survive.

A ripping sound rended the air as another huge section of dock splintered and Clint turned toward the South lot. He hurried toward it, past the warehouse shimmying like Mary's Jell-O salad after she served the first slice.

The further inland he walked, the more the ground beneath his feet vibrated. It shook with such an intensity, clumps of dirt and bits of rock visibly hopped.

The whole earth was a pan of popcorn sizzling and jumping over a fire. Clint's shoes sunk into the ground and he half-walked, half-crawled toward the rally point, using three points of contact with the ground. Ahead, between Clint and the parking lot, a giant section of the ground broke apart.

Scrub brush lining the parking area disappeared into the dirt like a hand reached up from the center of the Earth and yanked them down. A truck loaded with oversized wash tanks slid into a newly formed ravine. Someone standing by their vehicle shouted. Clint recognized the yellow emergency vest and the thick, bushy beard. Jack, his designated coordinator at the lot, motioned for him to hurry.

Everything is fine. Everyone is doing what they are supposed to. He told himself this over and over as he picked up the pace, struggling to make his way across the dirt and rocks. He clambered over broken bits of ground, slipping and sliding in the newly exposed earth. Another jolt and the ground ten feet ahead fell a handful of feet. The entire coastline was crumbling into the ocean.

He dug his nails into the new cliffside and pulled himself forward. If he didn't get over this ledge and onto solid ground, he might be swept out to sea with the dock and the barge and all the logs. He thought of Mika and he scrabbled to find a solid bit of asphalt to hold onto. The earth shook again and under his fingers, bits of parking lot disintegrated in his hand.

"Here! Grab this!" A red rope landed to his right and Clint reached for it, straining to keep purchase. His hand wrapped around the nylon as the ledge beneath his feet gave way.

He held on, both hands now clinging to the braided bit of rope as someone above him pulled. The toes of a pair of worn work boots appeared in Clint's vision and a thick, solid hand reached down to pull him up. He landed on the edge of the parking lot, dirt coating his entire front, and sucked in a breath.

Jack towered above him, blocking the full strength of the sun. He stared down beneath heavy brows. "You okay?"

"I am now." Clint squinted up at him. "Thanks for the hand."

"You're welcome."

Clint rested his head on the ground and closed his eyes. It took him a full minute to realize the ground had stopped shaking.

The earthquake was over.

CHAPTER SIX
MIKA

"Do you feel that?" Hampton asked, eyes so wide her lashes brushed her eyebrows.

"Feel wh—" Mika's question cut mid-word as the van shimmied sideways. She lifted in the seat, seat belt digging into the fleshy spot above her hip before another shift of the van sent her careening into the window. Her head banged into the glass and a rainbow burst across her vision.

Clutching the tender spot of her scalp, she shot a look of contempt at Ms. Rogers. *Oh.* Ms. Rogers gripped the steering wheel like a rodeo rider gripped a bucking bull's reins, skin taut and white. Fear sucked her cheeks tight to her teeth and paled her usual rosy glow into something sallow and sick.

"What's happening!?" A girl shouted behind Mika.

Hampton dumped her lunch into her lap and used the paper sack to breathe.

"It's okay." Mika gripped Hampton's thigh and

squeezed. "It's going to be okay." She tried to convince herself as much as Hampton, hiding her fear with earnestness, but a warble gave it away.

The tires rumbled as if they were running over rutted-out gravel and the brakes squealed. Mika craned her neck to catch a glimpse of road. Smoke billowed up from underneath the van. She buzzed the window down and the stench of burning rubber assaulted her nose.

"Ohmygod! What's happening?" The words rushed out of Hampton's mouth all mushed together, her breathing labored.

"Don't have a panic attack."

"How are you *not* having a panic attack?" Hampton gasped between fat gulps of air.

Mika wondered the same. Her heart fluttered, sweat slicked her palms, and if she didn't concentrate on breathing, she might pass out. Panic? Yeah, it was there all right, growling deep in her belly and growing louder by the second. But what good would it do to give in?

The van lurched and she fought down a wave of nausea.

"I'm l-losing grip on th-this thing." Words tripping over Ms. Rogers's tongue.

"We need to turn around. Get back to level ground." Ms. Chalmers twisted around to stare at the girls.

The shoulders of the two in front of Mika and Hampton were bouncing up and down. One cried out, "What's happening? Why won't you tell us?"

"We're in the middle of a damn earthquake, that's

what's happening!" Ms. Rogers, in her terror, forgot the 'no swearing' rule.

All at once everything made sense. The vibrations, the rumble beneath the tires, the smoke as Ms. Rogers tried to keep the van in the lane. Another tremor sent the van skidding across the asphalt, dangerously close to the edge of the road. Mika's head swam.

"Turn around!" Ms. Chalmers cried.

"Are you crazy? We need to get higher up," Ms. Rogers contested.

"Higher up the mountain?" Ms. Chalmers scrambled for the grab bar as the van swayed. "That's crazy!"

Mika stilled as the two troop leaders continued to squabble. Neither troop leader had ever been anything other than calm and collected. Even when Rachel lit her hair on fire stoking the flames, Ms. Rogers calmly tossed a bottle of water on the girl and Ms. Chalmers wrapped her in a towel. If they were panicked now...

She ran her tongue across her lower lip but it caught on a patch of dry skin.

"What else do you suppose we do?" Ms. Rogers asked. "If we can get to the summit, we might clear the quake. It might not reach the other—"

"We won't make it to the summit." Ms. Chalmers kept her voice low, but Mika still overheard. "If this keeps going, we'll be trapped under a landslide or worse."

"Landslide?" Ms. Rogers scoffed as if the idea was preposterous at best. "It hasn't rained in days. There's almost no snow on the peaks. There's nowhere for landslides to come from."

"If the quake is big enough, the ground will rip apart, wet or not," Ms. Chalmers argued. She sucked in a deep breath and blew it out in a steady stream. Her voice regained its even keel. "Just turn the van around. We'll have a fighting chance to make it down the mountain before it gives way."

Mika's pulse swooshed through her eardrums, pounding inside her head like the procession of a marching band. Hampton dug her nails into Mika's skin until her arm burned, but Mika didn't mind. It gave her something to focus on besides crushing fear. She tried to swallow, but her mouth lacked even a trace of spit.

"How am I supposed to turn around with the tremors bouncing me all over? I can barely keep going straight." Although she still protested, Ms. Rogers's voice lacked the defiance of before, as if she were ready to relent and do anything possible to keep from plummeting off the side of the mountain, van, troop, and all.

"Hug the higher side and we'll try to maneuver into a U-turn," Ms. Chalmers suggested, mimicking the movement with her hands.

Ms. Rogers's tongue poked from between her lips as she concentrated. She turned the wheel, bracing against the undulating ground. The back tires eased into the dirt along the side of the road and the van shimmied. Whatever traction they'd managed on the asphalt was gone.

Mika reached for Hampton's free hand and clenched her fingers around her best friend's palm. A girl behind them wailed a long, jagged sob. Clammy sweat loosened

Mika's grip and she reached up higher, clutching at Hampton's sweatshirt.

The rumble beneath the tires intensified, jostling the entire van. It shifted left, then right, then forward like the ground was one of those Magic Fingers machines she'd seen once in an old movie. A crack began to form, cutting across the road, ripping the white guidelines apart as the earth opened up. The van leaned, bottom half skidding across the dirt, the top half lifting off the ground.

Ms. Rogers froze in place, hands at ten and two on the steering wheel, paralyzed with fear. Ms. Chalmers unbuckled and leaned across the van, wrenching the steering wheel hard to the right. The van refused to cooperate, front wheels too far off the ground to gain purchase.

Mika's throat threatened to close and her stomach convulsed like the ground. Adrenaline pulsed through her veins and she turned to Hampton. "We've got to get out of this van."

Her friend stared at her in horror, unable to verbally respond. The voices and cries and blind panic around her receded and Mika focused on the feeling swelling inside her. The need to move, to find shelter behind a tree, away from the road, anywhere outside of the metal box they were trapped in, overwhelmed her. She reached for her seatbelt and released it as the van lurched violently.

Mika fell on top of Hampton. Sasha flew across the van like a rag doll, her book launching from her hands to hit the windshield. It was as if a giant had reached down from the clouds and picked up the vehicle, shaking it about to guess the contents.

Mika shut her eyes against the savagery of nature and willed herself to stay alert. If she didn't panic, she would survive. Hampton would survive. A sickening crunch popped her eyes open. A giant crack splintered across the windshield.

As she watched in disbelief, a rock the size of a softball hit the windshield in another place. Followed by another and another.

Ms. Rogers screamed.

A landslide.

Ms. Chalmers was right. Rocks and dirt and uprooted trees careened toward them, ripped from the ground from the force of the quake. It was like one of those slow-motion movies of snow-covered peaks where a skier attempts to beat the landslide down the mountain, only worse.

No one ever played the audio of those clips, did they? If they did, it would ruin skiing for everyone who watched it. *The noise...* it was part grizzly bear, part tornado, part end of the world all blended together on turbo speed.

Something massive collided with the van and Mika fell, landing hard on her back against the opposite window. All the air fled her lungs in a rush. A boot stepped on her hair and pain seared across her scalp.

Hampton screamed through clenched teeth, the sound leaking out like the cry of a dying animal. Mika's nose burned and tears pooled in her eyes. She willed herself not to cry. If she lost her wits, she might not make it off this mountain alive.

The landslide pounded the vehicle, gritty earth caving in on them straight out of an apocalyptic nightmare. She pressed her palms against her ears and shouted incoherent nothings until her throat ached. Her voice disappeared into the cacophony of terror swirling all around her.

She sucked in a pained breath and smelled gas and metal and the acrid tinge of urine. At last, the van's rear tires gave way and the entire vehicle and twelve occupants tipped over. A girl landed on top of Mika. Was it Julia? Sasha? She couldn't tell. A mass of blonde hair gagged her mouth and she fought for purchase against the window as the van slid a handful of feet. Someone screamed in her ear.

The van slipped again, a rough dive down another chunk of road, if there even was a road beneath them anymore. Mika wrapped her arms over her face and prayed they wouldn't sink into the earth and be swallowed up with the trees and debris barreling down from above. *Just let me survive this. Please. For my mom and dad. Don't let me die on the side of this mountain.*

Bile rose in Mika's throat, and she forced air through her nose to keep from vomiting. Something large and heavy slammed into the opposite side of the van, shattering the windows. Mika scrambled on her elbows, crawling toward the rear of the van and away from the broken glass and dirt flooding the cabin.

The vehicle shifted again, violently listing toward the

cliff as the metal dented and bulged from repeated impacts. Mika barely heard the rush of debris pelting them from all angles over the pounding of her heart. She risked another drag across the van, inching toward the rear, when another impact slammed the vehicle.

Something heavy and thick collided with her skull. A blinding pain pulsed through her temples, bulged her eyes. She gasped for breath as pain sizzled deep into her brain and everything snapped black.

"Have you had a chance to review the document marked as exhibit eight?" Don Lormack reclined in his chair like he hadn't a care in the world.

The witness swallowed so hard his Adam's apple bobbed. "Yes."

"Can you tell me what it is for the record, please."

"This appears to be a bank statement."

"Who's bank statement?" Lormack shifted almost imperceptibly, but Daphne caught it. The man had an amazing ability to appear calm and in control, even when an entire case hung on the answer to a single question.

The witness kept his eyes trained on the binder and the exhibit in question. "I don't know."

"You don't know. Are you sure about that, Mr. Crane? How about you look again."

"He's already answered—" Mr. Crane's attorney began.

"If you have a formal objection, make it. Otherwise, the witness is instructed to answer." Lormack waited.

Daphne held her breath.

"It appears to be a bank account out of Grand Cayman."

"Have you ever opened a bank account in Grand Cayman, sir?"

Mr. Crane cast a furtive glance at his attorney. "I don't see how this is relevant."

"I'll ask again. Have you ever opened a bank account in Grand Cayman?"

"Objection, asked and answered."

Lormack leaned forward. "I've asked, but he hasn't answered."

"Yes, he has." Mr. Crane's attorney sat a bit taller in his chair. "You might not like the answer, but he's answered."

"Not to my satisfaction."

"That's not for you to decide."

"We aren't leaving here until he answers this question."

"Like I said, he's already answered."

"Answer the question, Mr. Crane." He waited again, staring the man down across the burnished oak.

"Uh... um..." Mr. Crane began to mumble.

His attorney interjected. "I'd like a moment to speak with my client."

"No. You're not going to take a break and find a way to weasel out of this, Henry."

"Don, that's not what I'm doing and you know it. He has a right to take a break. We're taking a break."

"No, we're not. You have a problem with it, get the judge on the phone. Otherwise, he's answering the question."

Mr. Crane's attorney sagged into his seat, visibly beaten. "Can you repeat it, please?"

Lormack turned to the stenographer and waited. She scrolled the paper on her machine. "Mr. Lormack: Have you ever opened a bank account in Grand Cayman, sir?"

Before the man answered, a ruckus rose up from outside. What sounded like a million dogs all began barking and whining and carrying on. Don cut a steely glance in Daphne's direction.

She jumped out of her chair and peeked through the blinds. "It's the doggy daycare next door, Mr. Lormack. They're all in the yard, running in circles and barking at the air."

"Well, somebody get on the phone and shut them up!" Lormack glowered at the junior associate only allowed in the deposition as long as he kept his mouth shut and his pen ready. The young man scurried out of the room like someone set his chair on fire.

Lormack tugged on the lapels of his overpriced suit jacket. "As I was saying—"

The dogs grew louder, barks turning to whines and growls and growing increasingly frantic. It wasn't normal. Sure, there had been moments ever since the place opened last year when they'd had to call and ask for the dogs to be brought inside. But it was rare. And the animals never sounded like this. If Daphne didn't know better, she would think they were being tortured.

As she stared out the window, the skin on the back of her neck prickled. The blinds beneath her fingers quivered. At first, she blamed it on the stress, a tremble in her own hand brought on by being late and Lormack's bad attitude. But when the pen rolled off the table and landed at her feet, she blinked in alarm.

"You guys felt that, right?" The stenographer asked no one in particular, her eyes wide behind blue-framed glasses.

Daphne stepped away from the window. Her breath hitched as what felt like a vibration rumbled beneath her feet. She glanced at the stenographer. They both felt it.

Lormack seemed unfazed. He glared at the witness as if all the unforeseen disturbances were a creative attempt to stall. "You still have an unanswered question, Mr. Crane."

"Don, come on. You had to feel that," the man's lawyer interjected.

"All I feel is the complete lack of understanding what *under oath* means."

A distant roar of what sounded like thunder echoed through the room and the entire building shook. It wasn't supposed to rain, was it? Daphne glanced at the table. The water in the witness's glass trembled.

"Mr. Lormack, I don't think—" Daphne began.

He didn't even look at her. "I don't remember asking a paralegal for an opinion. If I remember correctly, there's still a question on the table."

The lights flickered.

Daphne took a step toward the door.

"That's it!" Opposing counsel grabbed his legal pad and reached beneath the desk for his briefcase. "This deposition is suspended."

"What?" Lormack practically roared in protest. "This is *my* deposition and I'll be the one to decide when it's suspended."

"In case you haven't noticed, there's a damn earthquake going on, Don. Unless you think my client is the one shaking the entire office."

"I wouldn't put it past him at this point."

As soon as the last word left his lips, the giant conference table lurched across the floor. Unoccupied desk chairs scattered. Daphne gasped and reached for the wall, stumbling as the building began to shake in earnest.

The cabinet, apparently unsecured to the far wall, danced across the floor, doors opening and closing as if on timers. Opposing counsel and his client leapt to their feet and staggered toward the exit. The attorney fell into a rolling chair as it careened in front of him. The client didn't even turn around.

Cracks began to form in the drywall, splintering like fingers of a dry creek bed suddenly brought to life. The stenographer screamed as the windows flanking the far side of the room shattered, sending bits of glass cascading to the floor.

Daphne's own voice failed her, throat swollen with panic.

She stumbled backward, away from the glass littering

the floor and the chairs and the desk. The conference table skidded across the room, propelling the stenographer backward in her chair and practically pinning her to the far wall.

Daphne found her voice at last and screamed. "We have to get out of here!" Over the din of the noise—from the dogs to the building breaking apart to the sound of mass chaos outside—no one heard her. Her voice sounded hollow and small.

Insignificant.

Her boss cursed and finally stood, grabbing his laptop off the broken table as a ceiling tile crashed into the room. Wires dangled from the ceiling and the power flickered once, twice, before failing completely. With the blinds mostly closed, the room descended into twilight and Daphne tripped over a heap of binders on her way to the door.

Something thick and solid collided with her shoulder and she screamed before ducking down, arms hugging her head in defense. She curled into a ball, crawling across the carpet in the direction of the door.

Another piece of the ceiling collapsed, breaking apart into a cloud of debris as it hit the conference table. Daphne tucked her nose into her elbow to ward against the dust tickling her nostrils and scratching her throat. She ducked beneath the thick slab of dark-stained desk and scanned the dim room.

Don stood ten feet away, attempting in vain to pluck his laptop and his briefcase off the floor. Every time the building shifted, he lost his balance and dropped one or the other. He bellowed out a curse as a chair careened across the open space and rammed into his backside.

Daphne twisted to catch sight of opposing counsel or the witness. They were nowhere to be seen, the only evidence of their existence an open door leading to the hall. She thought about all the earthquake training she'd had as a kid growing up in California. The safest place inside a building was an interior hallway away from any windows.

Her knees burned as she pushed herself across the carpet beneath the table. Outside, in the hall, a strobe light flickered, some useless emergency warning system telling her what she already knew: they were screwed.

This wasn't one of those little tremors they would all joke about the next day before the deposition resumed. This was a big one. How long had the building been shaking? A minute? More? It seemed like eternity.

She inched beneath the table, scooting past abandoned exhibits and broken chunks of drywall toward the door. The sight of a binder almost made her laugh. How inconsequential the morning now seemed. How unimportant.

A violent tremor rocked the building. Something collapsed on the floor to her right. An object rolled across the floor.

A high heeled shoe.

She swallowed, hard, and kept moving. Three feet to the door, then two, then one. Daphne slithered out of the room and into the hall. She peered around. Safe was relative, she supposed. There wasn't any furniture to slam her up against a wall or glass to shatter, but the wall was cracked, wires dangled from the collapsed ceiling, and a haze of dust and particulates hung thick in the air like fog rolling in off the coast.

She couldn't stay there. The building felt like it was ripping apart. She pulled her blouse up over her nose to block the worst of the dust hanging in the air and turned left and right. *Finally.* The sign for the stairs. Maybe she could make it outside to stand in the middle of the street and pray to God the ground didn't open up and swallow her whole. She staggered toward the door, slamming into the left wall before the building shifted and she tumbled into the right.

It seemed like she made no progress, the quake shoving her back every time she took a step. A sob clogged the back of her throat, mixing with the dust. Maybe she could hunker down, crouch in the hall and survive.

Visions of Mika and Clint finding her dead, crumpled in a heap where she'd given up, swam in her mind and she pushed herself off the wall. *I can do this. Only ten more feet.*

The door loomed before her and she reached for the handle. It slipped from her sweat-soaked grasp and she tried again, this time grabbing tight. The handle turned and Daphne tripped over a chunk of wall as she half-fell into the stairwell. It was dark and dry and blissfully without drywall or ceiling tiles or furniture.

She turned and braced herself against the door, pushing it closed with all her might. It slammed shut and for a moment, Daphne didn't know what to do. Her heart slammed against her ribs and her jagged breaths echoed against the bare walls. Plunged into darkness, with nothing around her but a trembling mass of concrete and steel, she slid to the floor, wrapped her arms around herself, and prayed.

Cherise emerged from the designated shelter area in the center of FEMA Region 10 Headquarters and sucked in a deep breath. "I clocked about four minutes. Anyone else?"

"Same." Derek ran a hand over his bald head and blew a steady stream of air from puffed cheeks. "That's magnitude nine, right?"

"I think so." As Regional Director, Cherise oversaw FEMA's disaster response for four states: Alaska, Idaho, Oregon, and Washington. Their headquarters—a squat, concrete square of a building—was built to survive a megathrust quake and it appeared to have done so with flying colors. The rest of the Western half of the state wouldn't be so lucky.

The low-level lights powered by the backup generator cast the office in an eerie, artificial glow. "Let's get back online as quickly as possible. If the quake was as bad as we fear, there's catastrophic damage all along the coast. Seattle, Tacoma, and Portland will be hardest hit due to size, but many smaller towns were probably destroyed."

"Should I pull up the forecasts?" Kelly, a younger FEMA hire responsible for modeling spoke up from the back of the assembled group of employees.

"Yes, let's refresh everyone's recollection on what we're facing." Cherise smiled out at the sea of people who would now spend every minute of the next few weeks together, working around the clock. "Everyone take a second, call or text home. Let them know you're safe, but you're here for the foreseeable future."

A brief complaint rumbled through the gathered employees and she held up a hand. "I know it's never the best time for a disaster, but that's why they pay us the big bucks, right?" Humor was necessary in times like these.

"Is there overtime at least?"

"Yes, and hazard, pay, too." Cherise flashed a conciliatory smile. "After you talk to your families, let's hit the phones. Run down your list of contacts, start figuring out where we stand. If we just survived what I think we did, there's not much time."

Everyone dispersed and Cherise hurried to her desk. Apart from scattered pens and a broken picture frame, everything appeared in working order. If only the rest of the region could be so lucky. She picked up the phone and called the first office on her list: Washington state's governor.

Out of place smooth jazz played on the line as the receptionist pushed her through.

"Hello?"

"Mr. Governor, it's a pleasure. This is Cherise McNeil, director of FEMA Region 10. Are you in a safe location?"

"Heck if I know. The whole building shook so hard I lost a filling."

"Do you have access to a helicopter, sir?"

"Well, yes, I assume so. Why?"

Cherise cut to the chase. "The incoming tsunami, sir. Based on our prior estimates, you have less than thirty minutes until Olympia will flood."

A string of curses filtered across the phone line. "Are you sure?"

"No. But it's been forecast as probable. Do you remember last year's briefing?"

"Might as well have been a lifetime ago." The governor's voice grew muffled as he spoke to someone else in the room. "Okay. I've put in the request. What else can you tell me?"

Cherise inhaled and began to recite the litany of facts she knew by heart. "At this point, the electrical grid has failed pretty much up and down the entire coast. All of Seattle and Portland are without power, most likely Tacoma as well."

"Tell me something I don't know."

She ignored his comment and plowed ahead. "There is mass destruction throughout the region, collapsed buildings, shattered glass. Up to seventy-five percent of all buildings in the Cascadia Subduction Zone have most likely collapsed. Half of all highway bridges are impassable. Half of the police stations are destroyed, along with two-thirds of all area hospitals and a third of all fire stations."

The governor swore.

"Landslides are most likely occurring throughout the region. We don't have any actual data, but prior estimates were as high as 30,000 in the Seattle area alone. Fifteen percent of Seattle is built on what scientists term liquefiable land. Meaning that during a megathrust quake, the ground will start behaving not like a solid, but a liquid, and anything on top of it will collapse."

"What's built on that fifteen percent, do you know?"

Cherise swallowed. "Seventeen day care centers and homes housing over 34,000 people."

Someone else's voice carried across the line and the governor responded from far away, "Give me one minute." His voice returned, urgent and full of fear. "Chopper is ready. What else do I need to know?"

There were a million more facts Cherise could relay. How the Pacific Northwest's critical energy infrastructure ran through the subduction zone and was most likely broken beyond repair, triggering fires and pipe failures and dam breaches. How most grocery stores were either ruined or without power. How the refugees would soon overwhelm any area volunteer services. But there was only one thing worthy of the moment.

"When the tsunami comes, you better be far out of the area if you want to survive."

"God help us. Thank you, Director."

The line went dead and Cherise closed her eyes for a moment before dialing the next number on her list.

"Ma'am?"

Cherise turned to find one of the lower-level employees she didn't personally know standing in front of her, lips gaping like a fish out of water. "What is it?"

"I just hung up with someone from Oregon Coastal Management."

"And?"

The employee moved her lips but no sound came out.

"Spit it out, hon, we don't have all day."

"He said due to the nice weather this weekend, he estimates there are 80,000 people on the beaches, ma'am." The young woman pushed her glasses up her nose. "Tourists, mostly. They won't have a clue what's coming or where to go."

Visions of beach goers running for their lives as a thirty-foot tidal wave crashed to the ground filled Cherise's mind, but she shoved them away. Tourists weren't the only ones about to die. "The inundation zone will probably encompass over a hundred thousand square miles and 453 miles of coastline. The beaches are the least of our worries."

The young woman staggered back a step and Cherise softened her tone. "It's going be more terrible than any of us can imagine. So get back to work."

She checked her phone for the time as the employee scurried away. Ten minutes post-quake. The water must be sucking away from the coastline already. She turned to the room and spoke over the din. "Anyone have eyes out there?"

One person held up a hand. Derek Tupper, the Assistant Director. "I've got City of Seattle's emergency management office on the line. They've confirmed loss of power and displacement. They lost their whole office! Complete collapse."

"Put it on speaker."

Derek hurried over, cell phone in his outstretched hand. "I've got the director here; can you tell us a little about what is happening in real time?"

"It's a mess," the man yelled on the other end of the line. His voice crackled and broke apart.

Derek met Cherise's eyes. "Talk fast in case we lose you."

"I'm surprised there's a cell tower still standing," the man continued.

"You said you lost your office?"

"We lost the whole building. The ground just wouldn't quit shaking. First the lights went out, then the windows blew. Our receptionist was hit by a huge shard of glass. Blood everywhere. She was, oh, God—"

"Okay, focus," Cherise cut in. "We need data. How are the roads?"

"What roads? Everywhere I look, the asphalt is torn apart. Huge cracks everywhere, chunks sticking up here and there. Monstrous holes where lanes used to be."

"What about landslides?"

"Not right here, but we're in a congested area. Mostly buildings, or what's left of them."

"You need to try and get to higher ground. You don't—"

A frightened scream echoed across the line, followed by garbled static. An exploding boom ruptured through the phone speaker. The line went dead.

"He's gone," Derek's voice flatlined. "We lost the line."

Cherise pressed her fingers against her lips. There was nothing their office could do for all the people suffering right now. The ones injured, trapped, half buried in debris. Those who survived the quake unscathed but didn't know to run. If they were anywhere close to sea level—like much of Seattle, the coastline, and countless tiny towns—they were about to be buried in a tidal wave of water.

It wasn't FEMA's job to protect people or to save them. It was FEMA's job to recover. Render aid to those who survived and get the affected areas back on their feet. It was a strange business; witnessing destruction and standing by, waiting until it was over to spring into action. But it was their job and they would do it to the best of their ability.

If their work over the next few weeks saved even a few lives, it was worth it. It would all be worth it. Cherise sent up a silent prayer for all those in the tsunami's path and returned to her job. There would be no sleep while all those souls perished and suffered. No breaks. No relief. They would help as many as they can for as long as necessary.

She dialed the next number and waited for it to ring.

"Are you sure everyone is here?" Jason ran a hand through his sweat-slicked hair as he stared out at the congregation of terrified employees.

"We're missing Sydney. She should have been at reception, but when I checked she wasn't there."

"I thought I saw her?" Jack spun around, picking off each employee in the air with his finger as he spotted them. "Guess I was wrong."

Clint brushed a clump of dirt off his shirt and turned to Jack. "We can do a walk around. Maybe she went straight to her car."

"Maybe she took off. Doesn't she have a little one with a sitter?"

"Ever since her mom passed away last year, yeah. One of the women I crochet with runs a daycare out of her house. I recommended her." Mary pressed her lips together. "She's right on the coast."

Jack's expression turned grim. "Let's check for her car."

Clint nodded and they took off, both looking for Sydney's small gray sedan. It didn't take long to confirm it was missing from the lot. "She must have left as soon as the quake started."

"Let's make sure." Jack pulled out his phone and brought it to his ear. A moment later it connected. "You all right?" He listened. "What about Addie?" His shoulders slumped in relief. "A text would have been nice."

A small voice echoed on the line. Clint closed his eyes for a moment. Everyone survived. It was practically a miracle.

"I'm sure he will be mad, yeah," Jake offered to Sydney on the phone. "You broke protocol. He'll probably put it in your file."

Laughter crackled.

"Well, I'm just glad she's safe." Jake waited. "You, too." He ended the call and turned to Clint. "Just like we thought. She bailed as soon as the pens on her desk started vibrating. Addie is fine. A little bit shook up, but the house made it through. She said the garage is toast, though."

Clint ran a hand through his hair and bits of dirt and grit clung to his palm. "At least she's okay. I can try to smooth it over with Jason. No need for her to get in trouble for it." They headed back to the group and confirmed Sydney was alive and well.

Other employees were marveling over the quake.

"I can't believe the warehouse survived." Mary covered her collarbone with one hand, overwhelmed by the experience. "It's a miracle if you ask me."

"It's steel beam construction," Clint offered. "If it didn't survive, nothing would."

Beth, the woman from the Port Commission office, held a broken high heel in one hand and her cell phone in the other. She pulled it down long enough to address the gathered Port employees. "Until we check with the businesses, yacht club, and marina, we won't know if everyone survived. The Commission is responsible for everyone operating on government-owned property."

Jack turned to their boss. "We aren't responsible, though, right?"

Jason pinched the back of his neck. "Not for evacuating, surely. But since we're mostly fine, Beth's right. We should fan out, start canvassing. Emergency services will have their hands full."

"Give me five minutes, will you?" Clint stepped away and called his daughter. If the troop van left on time, the girls should be near their camping area by now, over 4,000 feet in elevation. *Straight to voicemail.* Panic swelled momentarily until he remembered. *Right.* He forgot about the no phone policy.

Clint searched his email for the number of the troop leader, Ms. Rogers. He dialed and waited. It rang and rang until her voicemail picked up. Maybe they were out of cell range. Or she might be on the other line, calling worried parents. If she approached the task like Clint would have, then the Redshaws would be far down the alphabetical list.

He pulled up the Find My Phone app and waited for it to load. Nothing. He tried again. Maybe the cell towers were overloaded, or the troop was out of range. Cell service in the Park was spotty at best.

He shoved the phone in his back pocket as his thoughts hung for a moment on Daphne. With her new place in Bellevue and a fancy big-city job, she didn't have time for Clint and their small town. She hardly had time for their daughter. He kept hoping it was a phase—a mid-life crisis she would snap out of eventually—but now...

Was she even alive? How far did the quake spread? How many buildings in Seattle and Bellevue were now rubble? He shoved the thoughts aside. He didn't have time to worry about Daphne now. He had to think about Mika and the Port and ensuring everyone was safe.

He turned to Jason. "I can take a walk and start canvasing the logging companies. As soon as we're sure there's no emergencies, I'd like to head out. Find my daughter."

"Isn't she at school? I'm sure they did their earthquake drill and are going to notify parents about pickup soon. That place is fortified like Fort Knox."

"School's out." Clint grimaced. "Three-day weekend for teacher in-service. She's on a Girl Scout camping trip just up Hurricane Ridge."

Jason's eyes widened. "Gotcha. You can head out now if you need. We can handle the rest."

Clint exhaled in relief. Now that the immediate

disaster was over, at least for their facility, he wanted Mika by his side. "My truck's on the other side. I'll swing by the dock and make sure there's no visible emergency and head out."

Jason nodded his thanks.

"Don't fall in. I'm not rescuing you again." Jack grinned at him and Clint rolled his eyes.

"Sure thing." He wasn't planning on another death-defying stunt today if he could help it. He pulled up his recent dials on his phone and called Ms. Rogers again as he walked. This time the call failed to connect. He shoved the phone in his pocket and picked up the pace.

The Strait of Juan de Fuca glistened in the distance as he approached. Ninety-six miles in length, the Strait connected the Salish Sea to the Pacific Ocean. Thanks to the landslide, the new coastline wasn't visible: the ground abruptly ended short of the destroyed dock. Chunks of concrete and asphalt towered above the land, their bottom halves presumably wedged deep into the sand.

The log barge listed hard to port but it didn't appear beyond repair. With any luck, the timber company would successfully navigate the barge to a functioning port somewhere nearby, Vancouver perhaps, and recover most of their investment. Clint hoped the men working took heed of his warning and sheltered somewhere safe.

As he approached, a frown tugged his lips. *What the —?* The ship tipped, leaning even farther to port, as if the strait were pulling it away from the shore. Logs slipped through the metal supports holding them in place and splashed into the water. He quickened his steps, half jogging toward the new cliffside.

Five feet from the edge, he stuttered to a stop. With the collapse of the land, he'd expected some muddy debris, maybe some residual waves from mild aftershocks peppering the area. But he didn't expect this.

It was as if the entire Strait were being sucked out to sea. Waves of water slammed against the barge, pushing it further toward the Pacific Ocean. Half of the concrete piers still standing were bone dry with bits of seaweed and plant life clinging to their bases.

Clint blinked. Water used to crest fifteen feet high in the same places. The collapsed dock wasn't submerged in water but sticking out of the sand in jagged clumps.

What was happening? Had the earthquake rended the ocean floor apart? Was water being sucked to a new depth? He'd never heard of such a thing.

Then it hit him. *Oh, no. Oh, God, no.*

Horror rushed over him, not in a creeping mist, but in a giant, rolling wave of water.

The ocean floor hadn't opened up. The water was being sucked out to sea to create something that would destroy not just the Port, but the entire town. *A tsunami.* They had mentioned such a possibility in passing a few times during earthquake drills, but the possibility was so remote, they hadn't prepared. Only an earthquake of unimaginable magnitude spawned tsunamis. They'd all assumed if a quake like that occurred, they'd all be dead.

But there it was: undeniable proof. The water of the Strait pulled farther and farther away from shore, sucking at the sand, and exposing buried rocks and crabs and flopping fish. If this was happening in the Strait, then the coastline further south must be rapidly retreating.

Sandy beaches where tourists flocked during days just like this one were doubling, tripling in size. Would anyone there even know what was happening? Would swimmers be able to make it back to shore?

He thought about the house boats in the bay. The people who lived full-time on the water. Were they suddenly beached? Would they know to run?

Clint shook his head to clear his mind. Running. That's what they all needed to do. He turned on his heel and took off, heading straight back to the parking lot. No getting caught this time, struggling for his life, while the rest of his coworkers went about their business unaware. He would warn them. He would get them out.

He thought of Mika. If his daughter survived the earthquake, then she was far safer hiking to a campsite over 4,000 feet in elevation than anyone in Port Angeles. At only thirty-two feet above sea level, the entire town was about to be consumed.

CHAPTER TEN

MIKA

Every muscle in Mika's body ached. A thick, throbbing pain radiated across her scalp and neck, as if she'd slept wrong. Her eyelids sagged, weighed down with grogginess. After several failed attempts, she peeled one eye open and then the other.

Something wasn't right. "Hamp?" She called out. "Hampton?"

Blood coagulated in a small pool beside her head, soaking into the fabric ceiling of the van. Pockets of memory returned. The earthquake. The landslide. The crash.

She struggled to push her body off the ceiling, but a wave of dizziness forced her back. Air rattled into her lungs as she sucked in a breath. Her ribs ached with effort. She laid there, scrunched in an awkward ball in the rear of the upside-down van, for what seemed like forever. At last, her vision stopped spinning.

A branch pierced the van's destroyed side window

and Mika reached for it, using it as a support to drag herself to a sitting position. The van spun, but only in her mind. She closed her eyes to steady herself and beat the nausea back down. *I'm alive, and that's something.*

She called out again. "Hampton? Ms. Rogers?" Her voice echoed in the silence. Straining to listen, she waited, breath held, for any response. When none came, panic rose in her chest. She opened her eyes, blinking hard against the pain and terror.

A shaft of light lit the front of the van where an arm dangled loose and limp. Mika's mouth fell open in shock. *Ms. Rogers.* Her body hung from the driver's seat, blonde hair matted dark with blood.

A scream shot through Mika but died in her throat. "Hello? Is anyone alive? Can anyone hear me?"

Nothing. She crept forward, inching through twisted hunks of metal, ripped apart seats, and broken glass. As her knee slid forward, the van shifted, ceiling buckling beneath her weight. She stifled another scream.

Tears burned behind her eyes. Swallowing grew labored and painful. *Don't lose it. You're going to be okay.* She sucked in a lungful of air and eased forward again, reaching for the last row of seats.

Two girls hung from the seats, seatbelts working overtime against their lifeless forms. Brown hair hung in clumps, obscuring their faces, but Mika recognized the clothes. "Julia? Emma?"

She reached out, fingertips brushing Emma's arm. No response. She fumbled for the girl's wrist, searching for a pulse. Nothing. She dropped the arm. It fell like a hunk of meat, swaying in the dust-filled air. Mika steeled herself and reached up, pulling the girl's hair aside. A pair of lifeless blue eyes stared back at her, clouded over like those of a dead fish.

Shrinking back in horror, she let Emma's hair fall. Her back brushed something warm and she turned in a panic. Another Girl Scout. Another dead body. Blood oozed in a slow trickle down the girl's arm, dripping onto the ceiling.

Mika swallowed a thick wad of bile and kept moving, mouth mumbling words of some incoherent prayer as she reached the bench she'd shared with Hampton. She ducked forward, a quick check in case she couldn't bear the sight.

The seat was empty. No sign of her best friend.

Relief filled her, followed almost immediately by guilt and shame. Hampton might be alive, but no one else appeared to be. She checked the other girls, one by one, avoiding the obvious deaths—one girl with a compound leg fracture so severe a chunk of bone protruded from her thigh, one with a tree limb protruding from her chest like an alien explosion—until she reached the front.

Ms. Chalmers hung, arms twisted back behind her, neck at an angle Mika knew was broken. A deep gash in her forehead had already clotted, the blood dried and caked to her skin.

How long was I knocked out? Mika tucked her head between her knees and breathed, relying on the technique her father taught her years before. *If you're ever lost or hurt out in the woods, don't panic. Take a moment, center yourself. Focus on your breath.* She repeated his words in her mind, struggling to comprehend the situation.

She lifted her head at last. "Hampton?" Her voice sounded foreign. "Hampton, are you here?" With no reply, Mika crawled toward the shattered windshield, scooting between the dead troop leaders.

Mangled branches clogged the opening and Mika tried in vain to push a clump aside. She tugged and pulled and worked up a sweat, but it was no use. The van must have landed upside down in the middle of a thicket of dense, leafy bushes. She twisted around, steadfastly avoiding staring at the dead bodies beside her.

There had to be a way out. She searched for sky, finally catching a glimpse halfway down the van. In the row with Madison and ... the tree.

She pinched her eyes shut. *I can do this. I can do this.* Fear crackled in her chest, spreading like wildfire through her body as she thought of approaching the seat. She swallowed down a sea of nausea.

Inching closer, she reached out to grip the seat and pull herself between the rows. Madison hung upside down, pinned to the seat, eyes wide open and vacant, mouth in a perfect O. If it weren't for the six-inch wide tree trunk piercing her torso and the seat in front of her, Mika could pretend the girl was playing that face-freeze game they used to love as kids.

Only it wasn't a game. Madison was dead. Impaled as the landslide flipped the van off the road and into the forest.

Tears slipped down Mika's cheeks, softening dried tracks of blood as she crawled beneath Madison's lifeless legs dangling toward the ceiling. The tree had pierced the body of the van and broken when it flipped, ripping open a seam in the fabric and metal. She eased over jagged bits and chunks of foam, past Madison's blood-coated Converse, and toward the window.

The van shimmied as she crawled, an aftershock bouncing the wreckage to and fro. Mika bit her lip to keep from crying out. If she didn't get out of that van *soon*, she might not survive. A strong enough aftershock might send it careening down the mountain, dead Girl Scouts, Mika, and all.

At last, she reached the broken window. Pebbles of tempered glass littered the inside of the van and Mika used her sleeve to knock the few remaining pieces off the window frame. Wincing, she stretched her arms out in front of her, grabbed a piece of the bush crushed by the vehicle, and yanked herself free.

As soon as her thighs cleared the van, Mika began to slide through the branches and down what she rapidly discovered was the side of the mountain. She gasped, dirt and a stray leaf peppering her tongue, as she sought purchase.

With her whole body slipping out of the van like a limp rag doll, she scrabbled in the bushes, searching for something solid to hold on to. Bits of broken twigs escaped her arms as her fingers wrapped around a branch, thick and anchored to the ground. Her body bounced, once, twice, as her full weight stretched her arm. But she stilled.

She exhaled in relief, head resting in the thicket, until her arm grew numb from effort. Digging her toes into the dry earth beneath the bush, Mika managed to inch forward and find enough stability to rise up onto her knees. The van hung precariously, back end up in the air, tires slashed and sunning themselves. How had they not fallen even more?

She marveled at the relative luck. Of course she wished her fellow Girl Scouts and troop leaders were alive, but she'd survived. She was alive.

But Hampton?

Mika twisted in slow motion, one hand blocking the sun's haze, as she scanned the area. *There!* The hint of a bright yellow hoodie peeked out from behind the massive, muddy roots of an uprooted tree.

Mika barreled through the underbrush, slip sliding with feet weighed down as if clad in concrete shoes. Her thighs ached in protest, skin pricked with cuts and tears from ignored branches. But sheer determination banished the dizziness from her head wound, and for the first time since waking on the ceiling of the upside-down van, her mind cleared.

Hampton's alive. She must be.

The upended tree loomed, all mud and fibrous roots, and Mika eased around it. *Hampton.* She sprawled across the ground, arms flung wide, dirt and leaves collecting in her curls. Mika collapsed to her knees beside her best friend and searched for the tender spot beneath her jaw.

With two fingers, Mika pressed and waited. *Please be alive. Please.*

Yes! A faint pulse, weak, but steady. She cried out in relief. "Hampton! Hamp, wake up." Hampton didn't stir.

Tears clogged Mika's throat, but she tried again. Hampton had to wake up. She needed her. "Hampton. It's me, Mika." She choked out the words, her voice breaking at the end. "If you can hear me, please, twitch your fingers, blink, do something, anything."

She gave her a gentle shove and at last, a small groan slipped from Hampton's parted lips. "M-Mika?"

She fought the urge to scoop Hampton into her arms. What if she was injured? Broken ribs or worse. She thought about the classmate who survived a car crash the year before. The boy suffered a collapsed lung and a spiral fracture of his leg. He'd been in a wheelchair for weeks.

"Wh-What happened?" Hampton's voice came out scratchy and raw. She blinked, eyes cloudy and unfocused, brow knitting before she reached up with timid fingers to press her temple.

"You're alive," Mika cried, wiping tears away with the back of her hand. "It's me, Mika. You are alive, and so am I."

Hampton groaned again as she tried to raise herself to her elbows.

Mika gently helped her. "Be careful. Don't move too fast. Does anything hurt?"

Hampton shook her head but when she did, she yelped in pain.

"What is it?" Mika clutched her arm.

"My neck hurts. I feel like I was in a car accident."

"You *were* in a car accident. A van accident, actually."

Hampton's eyes wandered over Mika as if trying to focus. Her pupils were over-dilated for the amount of sun.

"Where are we?" Hampton blinked. "Where is everyone?"

Mika swallowed hard. How could she tell her friend everyone else was dead?

"Can you sit up?" She changed the subject.

Hampton palmed the back of her head, brows dipping in confusion. "I—I think so."

"Easy does it." Mika leaned over and helped Hampton sit.

"Everything is spinning. I feel sick." Hampton frowned into the dirt and blinked once, twice, three times. "I can't remember what happened."

Were those symptoms of a concussion? Mika didn't know, but Hampton definitely wasn't herself. She tried to keep it brief. "We were in an accident on our way up the mountain. On the Girl Scout camping trip, remember?"

"I told you this was a terrible idea." Hampton lifted her chin and squinted at Mika. "Where are we?"

Mika smiled despite the horror of the situation. Hampton might have a concussion, but at least she still had her humor. She fought the urge to wrap her in a hug. "On the mountain. There was an earthquake."

Hampton blinked in slow motion. "I think... I

remember. The van wobbled, right? A few times. You... held my hand, told me it would be all right."

Mika managed a rueful smile. "I guess I was wrong."

Hampton sat still, brain seemingly working in slow motion like it was buried in a vat of Jell-O. Mika would have to take it slow. "Can you walk?"

"I... don't know."

Mika stood and helped Hampton to stand, pulling her up an inch at a time until they stood side-by-side. Hampton swayed on her feet and Mika slipped an arm around her waist. "Is this okay? I'm not hurting you, am I?"

Hampton began to shake her head but froze as pain washed across her face. "No. It's fine."

With agonizingly slow steps, Mika led Hampton out of the undergrowth and to a relatively flat portion of ground dotted with ferns. She eased Hampton down onto a patch of dirt before standing back up. "I need to go back to the van to find the bag of phones."

"Where is it?" Hampton squinted against the sun, bringing a shaky arm up to shield her eyes.

"Past the tree roots about twenty feet. It got stuck in some thick bushes. I think that's what helped it finally stop rolling."

Hampton's face turned the color of dried paste. "It rolled?"

Mika nodded.

For the first time, Hampton looked around her, head swiveling in slow motion. "Where's everyone else? That girl with the paperback and the troop leaders?"

Mika's mouth opened but no words came out. Tears welled in her eyes as she stared past Hampton toward the wreckage. Grief tangled itself in her throat and she shook her head. A single tear leaked from the corner of her eye and she wiped at it, hard.

Hampton's face fell, and her chin trembled. "All of them?"

Mika nodded. "We're on our own. But it's okay. We just have to get down off this mountain and everything will be fine."

"How? We have no ride, and half the world is split apart. Look at it. It's all craters and cracks."

"I know, but we can't stay here forever." Mika hoped some of her resolve would rub off on Hampton. "If we can find the bag of cell phones, hopefully we can get a signal to dial out."

"What good will that do? A car or an ambulance can't make it up here. I don't even see the road."

Mika straightened her shoulders. "We'll call my dad. He'll find a way to come rescue us, Hampton. I swear it."

CHAPTER ELEVEN
DAPHNE

Daphne didn't know how long it had been since the building stopped shaking. She'd slid into a near-fugue state, repeating a handful of words in a simple prayer over and over. Asking for someone, anyone, to look after her husband and daughter. The two most important people in her world. The two she'd left behind.

Blood pounded in her eardrums, a steady *whoosh-whoosh* as she managed to suck in a decent breath. Was there even anything left of the building apart from the stairwell? She hadn't a clue. In the dark, she couldn't tell if there were cracks running the lengths of the walls or if half the stairwell had collapsed two floors below.

With no emergency lighting, the stairwell might as well be space. No light, no difference in shading between the air one inch in front of her face and the wall ten feet away. Daphne longed for her phone. Not to endlessly scroll like so many nights alone on her couch, but to beat back the cloying darkness.

After another few minutes of waiting, she forced her legs to unbend and support her weight. Her muscles ached in protest, knees knocking together. But she dug her fingernails into her palms and wobbled toward what she thought must be the door.

Her knuckles brushed something hard and unforgiving. The concrete wall. She uncurled her fingers and stretched them out, trailing fingertips across the wall, feeling the cracks running this way and that like veining in her favorite Gorgonzola.

The texture changed, trading dusted concrete for smooth metal, and Daphne wrapped her fingers around the door handle and pulled. Nothing. She pulled again, adding her other hand before lowering into a shallow squat and adding her legs for effort. It wouldn't budge.

Panic crawled up her throat at the thought of being trapped. How long would it take someone to find her? A day? Two? A sob escaped her throat and her grip slackened, but only for a moment.

Come on, Daphne. You're a fighter, not a quitter. She sucked in a deep breath and yanked on the handle again and the door shifted, bottom scraping open a fraction of an inch. Had the whole building shifted? Thrown the door frame out of whack?

She tried again, tugging and yanking, putting real effort in with her legs until the bottom of the door warped enough to catch a glimpse of light.

It streamed in, illuminating dancing motes of dust in a shaft of light no wider than an inch. But the sight made Daphne gasp. She bent down to a low squat and gripped the bottom of the door with both hands and pulled. It gave way with a creak and a groan, propelling her backward as it swung. She landed hard on her backside before rolling back and almost over.

Not the most graceful of escape attempts, but it didn't matter. Light bathed the stairwell and Daphne sobbed in relief. There was still something left of the building, at least.

She stuck her head into the hall as a broken ceiling tile wobbled and fell, just a hair's breadth away from her nose. Dust plumed into the air, and she covered her mouth with her elbow against the worst of the debris.

"Hello?" Her voice came out raw and squeaky. She cleared her throat and tried again. "Hello? Is anyone here?"

She scurried forward, dodging broken hunks of ceiling and wall, darting past exposed wires and bulging drywall. To her right, what looked like a half desk sliced the hall in half, exposing an empty conference room, shattered windows gaping in the sun.

"Hello?" She called out again.

More silence. Panic still pulsed through her body, but not like before. Instead of sharp and insistent, it lingered in the background like a nagging to do list or bland office music. She reached the large conference room where the deposition had ceased only minutes before.

"Hello?"

One glimpse inside and her knees buckled, refusing to cooperate. She clutched the door frame to stay upright.

Underneath the conference table, Don's mangled

body stretched from one side to the other, bent and twisted beyond the possible. She knelt near him, reaching to check for a pulse. His arms were twisted behind him, broken. As she leaned over, his face came into view, eyes wide open, unblinking and lifeless. He stared at the ceiling, mouth open in an exaggerated O, still terrified even in death.

The sight sent Daphne scurrying back on all fours, crawling like a crab away from him. She bumped into the back of a broken chair, its wooden shards poking into her scalp. She cried out and pushed away, tucking herself against the only undamaged portion of wall.

Another body lay face down, impaled by a twisted piece of metal. A chair leg, maybe? Tears slid down her cheeks, free, and unstoppable. Was she the only one to survive?

A faint noise rose from across the room and Daphne turned. Tucked against the far wall was the stenographer, blue shirt billowing over the conference table. Her head lolled to the side, but as Daphne stared, she swore she saw movement. "Hello? Are you alive?"

One of the woman's hands flapped and hope surged in Daphne's chest. She crawled across the floor, avoiding Don's dead, mangled body, and the worst of the debris. The stenographer was pinned, the table pressed tight against her midsection.

"It's okay," Daphne stammered in a weak voice as she rose up to find the woman conscious. "I'm here. I'll help you. Do you think you can move?"

"I think my ankle's busted." A violent cough shook

the woman's body. "And this table is too heavy to move. I called out before. When I didn't hear anyone—"

"Same." Daphne stood on shaky legs. "But we're alive." She gave the woman a tight smile. "I'm Daphne."

"Pamela." She coughed again. "You think you can help me move this table?"

"Of course." Daphne took a step back, bare foot narrowly missing a jagged piece of broken chair. "How about we try to tip it over? I don't think I can slide it. Not with all the debris."

Pamela nodded as she set her full lips in a line. "I don't know how much help I'll be."

"It's okay. Just watch out—maybe cover your face or lean back against the wall. I don't want to hit you as I tip it."

The stenographer did as Daphne suggested, bringing one arm up to shield her face as she pulled back as tight as possible against the wall.

With a deep breath, Daphne reached for the table, gripping the edge in both hands. She used her legs, pushing up from the bottom. The table lifted from the ground and Pamela cried out. Daphne ignored it, staggering forward under the weight and pushing up and up until at last, she reached the tipping point. Momentum carried the table over and it landed with a crash against the destroyed windows.

The stenographer sucked in loud, desperate breaths as she patted her midsection all over.

"Are you okay?"

"I think so."

"Good. Because we need to leave."

"What?" Pamela jerked her head up in alarm.

"The building might not be stable. It could collapse from the damage or an aftershock could crumble the remaining supports. We need to head outside, assess the damage, see where to go."

Pamela's round cheeks swelled as she trapped a breath inside her mouth and held it. "I'm no good on stairs. Even before my ankle. I've got a bad hip. Partial disability." She reached around on the carpet beside her, fingers swiping across the floor.

"What are you doing?

"Looking for my purse. We should call for help."

Daphne spun around, doing the same. Her purse should be there, somewhere.

"I'm not getting a signal."

She turned back around. Pamela held her phone in the air, waving left, then right. "There's nothing. Not even one bar."

"At least you have a phone." Daphne palmed her hips as she stared out at the debris. "I don't see my bag anywhere."

She eased over to the window, skirting past a collection of wrecked chairs conspiratorially gathered in the corner. The blinds were torn and hanging haphazardly across the open window and Daphne reached up with both hands and yanked them down. They fell in a crash and Pamela exclaimed behind her.

"Sorry." Daphne didn't turn as she apologized, focused instead on the sheer devastation now taking center stage in the bare window. The street undulated like a ribbon in the breeze, asphalt rising and falling more than ten feet up and down. The doggy daycare next door was flattened, warehouse nothing more than a heap of concrete blocks and crumpled metal roof.

Destroyed cars littered the street—some upside down, some on their side, one on fire. The six-story building across the street listed hard to the right, top two floors sliding into the parking deck and splattering the brick facade across the top. Destruction as far as she could see. Apart from their building, she didn't see a single one standing on its own.

She leaned out, scanning the street below, but retreated in an instant. She'd seen enough dead bodies for one day.

Daphne forced a swallow and turned around. "I don't think anyone is coming." The words hollowed her out from the inside, each one dumping the last of her hope on the floor between them.

Pamela held up a set of keys. "Found my purse. I was sitting on it. If the parking deck's intact, I've got a Jeep."

Daphne risked a glance behind her to the window. The deck was on the other side. "I took an Uber."

"If you can help me out of here, I'll give you a ride anywhere you want to go."

"Can you drive with that ankle?"

"Only one way to find out."

Daphne chewed on her lip. Pamela outweighed her by what, a hundred pounds? Would she even be able to help the woman stand? All the same, a ride was a ride.

Where else was she going to find a way out of this destruction?

She plastered a thankful smile on her face and nodded. "Sounds good. I'll help you up." With one arm roped around Pamela's waist, Daphne steeled herself. On the count of three, she lifted, straining against the other woman's weight. They wobbled, half-fell, and almost toppled over, but after a few agonizing moments, they managed to stand.

Pamela shifted, testing her ankle. As soon as she put weight on it, she cried out. "Don't think I'll be driving after all."

Daphne nodded. "We make it to your car and I'll drive."

Pamela agreed, and together they set off on the agonizing journey to the parking deck.

CHAPTER TWELVE
CLINT

Clint ran, waving his arms in a blind panic. No one noticed until he began to shout. "We've got to move! Now!"

He skidded to a stop, shoes sliding across the cracked parking lot, and he sucked in a lungful of air. "We've got to get out of here." He grabbed his pants in fists above the knees as he bent over, out of breath.

"What are you ranting about?" Jack screwed up his face and squinted. "Earthquake's over."

"The Strait is draining. Water is getting sucked out to sea. That's the first sign of a tsunami."

"What?" Mary's mouth fell open. "You can't be serious."

"I am." Clint managed to pull enough air into his lungs to stand. "Don't you remember that earthquake preparedness class a few years ago? They mentioned the worst case. Said if it's a monster quake, like this one I'm guessing, our biggest threat isn't the quake itself it's what comes after."

"The water."

"Exactly." Clint turned to stare out at the Strait, beautiful and sparkling from this distance. "It's already pulling away from the shore."

"We never prepared for that." Mary's voice came out small and tinged with fear. "Everyone told us if it happened, it was hopeless."

Jack wiped a hand across his mouth. "How long do we have?"

"I don't know."

"How big will the wave be?"

Clint threw up his hands. "Your guess is as good as mine."

Mary looked around the group in alarm. "What about our families? Our children? Hamilton Elementary is what, six or seven blocks from the coast?"

"I think there's a Montessori even closer." Beth pressed a hand to her cheek. "My husband works at the Medical Center. It's right on the water."

Clint motioned for everyone to stop. "We don't have time to be talking it over. If you've got a loved one in harm's way, call them. Try to warn them."

"What if we can't reach them?"

"Do your best." He glanced at Jason for approval. The man nodded, mouth hanging open in shock. "But focusing on them won't do any good if we don't get moving. Right here, on the Port, we're sitting ducks. Everyone needs to leave. If you drove, get in your car. Get to higher ground. If your house is far enough inland, go there. If not, I'd say head as far away from water as you can get."

"Which way?" Mary wondered.

"I'd say west on the 101. It curves inland. If the road isn't damaged, and it's still passable, that might be the best route."

"There's not much out that way," Jack pointed out.

"Exactly. All we have to do is survive the flood. It'll recede. We just have to wait it out."

Clint pulled out his phone and called Daphne. It rang and rang. She didn't pick up. He turned away from the group as her voicemail clicked on. "Hey Daph, it's Clint. If you're getting this, you need to get to higher ground. I don't know where you are, but water's coming. Fast. Seattle's gonna flood. Bad. Find a high rise or head east. Anywhere you can, as fast as you can." He hesitated. "Love you."

He ended the call and turned around. Jack gave him a knowing glance. "You alright?"

"I will be once we get everyone out of here." He clapped his hands for attention. "Everybody, let's move!"

Clint ushered the employees who were slow to react toward their vehicles. His boss didn't seem capable of springing into action—none of them did. Maybe it was the aftereffects of all the adrenaline leaving their bodies. Maybe it was because they hadn't seen the water, the horror of it all being sucked away. But they needed to move faster.

He helped Mary into her older Rav-4 and leaned

over the open driver's side, perching his arm across the top. "Where's your house?"

Her fingers shook and she struggled to shove the key in the ignition. "Near Peninsula College. It's up a little rise."

"Good. Head there. If you see the water coming, keep driving. Is Frank at home?"

Mary nodded. "Works out of the shed out back."

"Find him and make sure you're both out of the way." He shut the door and rapped on the hood.

Mary eased out of the parking lot, fourth in line behind other employees.

Clint checked the time. Where did the last ten minutes go? He turned toward the water. No sign of a wave, but that was meaningless. It was coming, he knew it.

A whistle caught his attention, and he twisted around to find Jack flagging him down. "Can I hitch a ride? I let Jimmie and a couple guys who work the dock take my truck since they rode the bus over this morning."

"No problem." Clint scanned the lot. Beth sat behind the wheel of a newer Lexus, painted nails tapping the steering wheel as she queued up behind an F-150. Besides his truck, only three other vehicles still sat empty. "Where's Jason?"

Jack lifted a brow. "Don't know. Thought he'd be gone by now."

Clint frowned. Ever since the quake, Jason had been out of sorts, failing to take charge while everyone around him panicked. Clint nodded toward the warehouse. "I'm gonna check it out. Make sure he didn't go back for something."

"But the water—"

Clint held up a hand. "It'll only take a minute." He tossed Jack his keys. "If you see the wave, blast the horn."

Before Jack argued, Clint took off, loping toward the warehouse door. He ducked inside and called out for his boss. "Jason? Mr. Rechio, you in here?"

Something clattered to the floor and Clint followed the noise past reception and toward the collection of offices flanking the rear of the building. He ducked inside his boss's office and found the man, arms buried in a banker's box.

"What are you doing?"

Jason twisted toward the file cabinet and grabbed a chunk of files before turning back around and dumping them into the box. "Our older accounts are still paper only. If we lose them, I won't know how to reconcile the budget. We'll be sunk."

"We'll be dead if we don't get out of here." Clint stepped forward. "We've got to go, now."

"Just a few more."

Outside, a horn blasted. Once, twice, three times. Clint rushed toward Jason. "That's Jack. It means the tsunami is here. Leave it."

Jason's eyes bulged. "But—"

Clint grabbed the man by the wrist and dragged him around the edge of the desk. "We don't have any more time."

The horn blared again outside and Clint pulled Jason

along, out of his office and down the hall. He burst through the door to reception and yanked Jason in front of him. The man half stumbled, half fell, into the exterior door and Clint shoved it open around him.

They emerged into the sun to a giant wall of water no more than a hundred yards away.

Jason stared in horror. "We're going to die."

"Not if I can help it. Run!" Clint took off, B-lining straight for his truck. Jack threw the driver's side door open and Clint launched himself into the seat. Jason followed seconds behind, climbing over the side of the pickup bed and falling in as Clint wrenched the gear shift into drive and slammed the gas.

The truck's rear wheels shimmied, kicking dust into a cloud behind them. The water gained, rising out of the strait like a blanket of wrath. He pressed the gas pedal to the floor and gripped the steering wheel so tight his fingers spasmed.

"We aren't going to make it." Jack stared out the rear window.

"Yes, we are." Clint kept his eyes on the road and off the impending doom behind him. The truck barreled out of the Port, bouncing over the curb as he passed the nicest restaurant in the area. Half of the facade lay in a heap on the sidewalk. A handful of people gathered at the open-air pavilion where the farmer's market set up every Saturday. He blared the horn. Waved at them to run.

The light in front of him turned red and Clint slammed his fist on the horn, relentlessly broadcasting their approach.

"There are vehicles, Clint. We can't—"

Clint floored it toward the intersection, narrowly missing an older woman in a Subaru. Up ahead, cars blocked the road. He glanced left and cranked the wheel, bouncing over the curb and into a gas station. Half of the awning above the pumps hung in an awkward arc, broken in the quake.

He swerved past a car parked at a pump, windshield broken from debris, and back onto the road, darting in between a propane truck stalled on the side and a woman standing on the sidewalk with her dog. He honked again and motioned toward the mountains.

All these people. They thought the earthquake was the worst of it. His heart tugged in a million directions. He had half a mind to stop, convince them to flee. But then he thought of Mika, only sixteen years old on the side of a mountain with a gaggle of girls. If Daphne was already dead... if she was about to be swallowed up by an onslaught of water...

Clint had to stay alive. He had to be there for his daughter. He risked a glance in the rear view. They'd gained on the wave, putting more distance between them and impending death than he'd expected. But it wasn't enough. He cranked the wheel, turning so fast onto East Eighth Street, the rear right wheel lifted off the ground. Jason scrambled over to the right side of the pickup bed, lending his weight to the lighter back end.

The truck fell back to the ground with a thud and Clint punched the gas, blasting past a series of medical buildings, all damaged to varying degrees, a coffee shop and way too many people. He slammed on the brakes.

Jack slid forward, head almost colliding with the windshield. "What the heck, man?"

Clint swallowed down a wad of bile. "I can't do it."

"Can't do what?"

"Leave everyone." He twisted around and peered out the back. "Where's the water?"

Jack twisted around and squinted. "I can't see it. Doesn't mean it isn't there."

He sucked in a breath and reached for the door handle. "Then we have a bit of time. Come on."

CHAPTER THIRTEEN
MIKA

The van groaned under Mika's weight as she wrenched on the upside-down rear door. A dent spanned the entire midsection of the back end, warping the latch. She tugged, but it got her nowhere.

Muttering a curse beneath her breath, something she saved for extreme situations, she tried again. Fingers wrapped around the handle, Mika pulled with all her might. Still nothing.

"Hampton?" She called out without turning around. "You think you could lend me a hand?" When her best friend didn't respond, she stepped back from the van and turned around.

Hampton stood off to the side, randomly plucking apart an uprooted fern. The longer she'd been awake, the more distant she'd become. Mika had tried to keep her in one place, away from the van and in relative safety, but she'd refused. Wandering off into the forest.

Mika called out, "Hamp? You okay?"

"My head hurts." She motioned to the rear left side. "All along here. Like a giant's squeezing it super hard."

"You probably hit your head when you flew from the van. Maybe you should sit down. Take it easy."

"I flew through the van?" Hampton brightened. "Like a superhero?"

Mika stilled. Did her best friend really not remember? Even if she blacked out during the crash, they'd just talked about it a few minutes ago. "The crash, remember?"

Hampton frowned at the plant in front of her and plucked off another section of leaves. "Hmm?"

A faint rumble reverberated beneath Mika's feet and she gave a start. Time wasn't on their side. She needed to find those phones and make contact with her dad. *Now.* She frowned at Hampton. "Just don't go anywhere, okay?"

Hampton didn't respond, still engrossed in dissecting the plant. Mika shoved her worry aside and clambered over exposed roots and chunks of destroyed tree to the nearest shattered van window. She managed to wiggle inside, this time without climbing over an impaled Girl Scout.

Everyone still hung upside down, suspended in some sick time loop of horror. Blood no longer dripped from open wounds, though, most of it now sticky and coagulating on the ceiling-turned-floor. She accidentally stepped in a puddle, tennis shoe squelching out a nauseating burp.

A rush of bile rocketed up her throat and she reached

for the van's wall to steady herself. *No throwing up now.* She had a job to do. With steadfast resolve, she avoided looking at the bodies all around, focusing instead on the hunt for the forest green nylon bag the troop leaders used to collect all the phones.

It has to be there. It just has to.

Carefully stepping here and there, dodging a dangling leg, a fallen shoe, a clump of... bloodied hair. *Oh, God.* Mika kept searching. Duffle bags, backpacks, a cooler full of food. But no nylon sack. No phones.

She cried out in frustration. If she couldn't find it, then how would her dad find her? How would he know where to look? She crouched to peer out the window wedged into the dirt and foliage. Hampton was right, they couldn't even see the road. Would someone even see it if they searched? Was the road further down the mountain even passable?

Her thoughts spiraled until a metal case slipped from a seat back and clattered at her feet, spilling a rainbow of colored pencils across the ceiling. The pencils bobbled about, turned into a pile of jumping sticks from another aftershock.

Metal groaned and the van pitched. Mika reached for the nearest thing to hold, and her fingers grazed a bare leg, skin cold and rubbery. She recoiled and regretted it in an instant, falling as the van shifted again, sliding a foot or two down the sloped grade.

Panic seized her. It had been easy inside the horror of the makeshift metal coffin to forget about the earthquake and focus on the after. But earthquakes never stopped with one. Aftershocks could be worse than the initial quake; she'd learned that in geology in middle school. Since the ground was already disturbed, a smaller aftershock could collapse buildings and ruin mountainsides that had survived the larger vibration.

She fell to her knees, scouring the van for anything to use. She wrapped her hand around the cooler and hoisted it toward her as the van shifted again. She fell, banging into the side of the van. Pain radiated across her knee and she pulled it up to find a gash an inch long blooming with blood.

No time to dwell.

After shoving the cooler out the nearest window, Mika crawled toward the troop leaders, grabbing the first backpack she found and hurtling it out the window. She found Hampton's pack as well and managed to shrug that on before canvasing the front one last time.

Ms. Chalmers stared at her, eyes open in fading horror, pupils clouded over and whites of her eyes turned blue. She shoved past the dead woman and popped open the glove box. A pile of maps tumbled to the ceiling and Mika scooped them up as the van groaned again.

Branches snapped as the vehicle shifted. Glass fell out of the windshield as the van slid away from its initial resting place. Mika's heart pounded like a war drum, demanding she run. She hated to leave without the phones. Where could they possibly be?

Another groan, another tremor, and Mika gave up, hustling toward a shattered window as the van slipped down another foot. A scream lodged in her throat. She scrambled toward freedom, fingers sifting through pebbled glass before digging deep in the earth outside.

She shimmied through, ignoring the two girls suspended above her and slipped out of the van as it slid again. The ruined frame grazed her calf as she inched free. "Hampton!" Mika shouted. "Are you clear?"

Mika crawled on hands and knees away from the wreckage. "Hampton!" Standing on shaky legs, she spied her friend, twenty feet away, waist-deep in ferns, hands running over a fallen tree covered in moss. "Hampton! You need to move!"

Her friend didn't respond. Didn't even turn.

Branches cracked beside Mika and ferns disappeared, swallowed up by the van as it slid again. If it picked up momentum, it would roll. And Hampton was right in its path.

Without a second's thought, Mika tore through the understory, trampling the pale pink and white blooms of oxalis spreading in front of her, breaking the tendrils of bright green ferns. Her foot slipped on a rock covered in moss and lichen and she banged her shin. The pain didn't register above the fear.

"Hampton! Hampton, damn it! Move!"

At last, her friend glanced up, confusion knitting the space between her brows. She held up a branch covered in clumps of white flowers. "I think I found a huckleberry bush. My mom's been trying to grow some in the backyard." She didn't notice the giant crushed vehicle slip-sliding in slow motion, flattening everything in its path.

Mika reached her as the van slammed into a fallen tree. It hovered, rocking back and forth in the air, until another rumble from deep in the earth tipped it forward. Mika watched in horror as the van began to roll.

Oh, no. Nonononono. She grabbed Hampton by the arm. "Come on, we have to move."

Hampton shrugged against her. "Get off me. You're getting dirt on my hoodie."

"We're going to die, Hampton! I don't care about your hoodie."

"That's not very nice."

Mika yanked on Hampton's arm. "Come on!"

Hampton cried out as Mika dragged her, one step at a time through the brush and out of the path of the oncoming disaster. "Stop it! You're hurting me!"

"Beats dying!" Mika kept going, tugging and pulling and fighting her best friend with all her might.

The van rolled once, twice, three times, before it gained enough momentum to increase speed. Mika grabbed Hampton's other arm with her free hand and threw her to the ground before collapsing on top of her. The van rolled past them, metal bending and warping, glass bits landing on their outstretched legs.

Mika sucked in a breath as the vehicle kept going down the mountain, back toward town. Twenty feet, then thirty, forty. She sat up, watching with wide eyes as it barreled straight for a massive, still-standing pine tree. On impact, the tree shook, giant branches raining needles. Something in the van broke and hissed.

A moment later, a boom echoed across the

mountainside and flames erupted from the rear of the vehicle. Mika struggled to her feet. All the girls inside. Her troop leaders.

But they were dead. She'd checked, then checked again.

She watched in a combination of awe and revulsion as the flames engulfed the vehicle and thick, black smoke billowed into the sky. She thought of Sasha and the book she'd never read again, of Madison and her infectious laugh. Of her troop leaders and their families back at home waiting for word.

They were all gone. Never coming back. A sob rose inside her, but the sound of retching pulled her back. Hampton hunched over, heaving into the moss.

"Are you okay?"

Her friend looked up, vomit dribbling down her chin. "I don'feelso... gooooood." Hampton's words came out slurred and thick.

Mika crouched in front of her and stared into her eyes. Her pupils were dilated, but not the same. One was fat and thick, almost eclipsing her iris, the other, half the size. What did that mean?

"Can you stand?"

Hampton didn't answer.

They needed to get away from the smoldering van, the smoke, and the debris. Find some place to shelter. Mika glanced up at the sky. With night rapidly approaching and Hampton so discombobulated, she needed to face the facts. They were roughing it in the woods tonight.

She chewed on her lip as she glanced at the spot where the van had been. The corner of the cooler popped out of the expanse of green and she spied a troop leader's backpack beside it. With any luck, they would have food and shelter and a means to camp for at least the night.

Mika tightened the straps on her backpack and smiled at her friend. "You stay right here while I go get the gear. Then we'll find a good spot to hunker down. Don't worry. Everything will be fine."

She said the last bit more for her benefit than Hampton's. Her friend's condition worried her. Was nausea and confusion a side effect of a concussion? What about her pupils and the slurred words? Mika sent up a quick prayer, begging for Hampton to be okay, but deep in her gut, her unease deepened.

CHAPTER FOURTEEN
TASK FORCE

A hastily made infographic of the Pacific Northwest filled the screen and Michael Urston, the 13th Administrator of the Federal Emergency Management Agency, ran the red dot of a laser pointer along the coast. "As you can see, the areas shaded red are those we believe suffered the worst damage in the quake, although reports are coming in off social media that areas as far south as Sacramento, California and as far east as the Idaho state line felt the tremors."

The President of the United States leaned back in his chair, steepling his fingers. "Casualty estimates?"

"From the quake itself? Unclear at this time."

"Give me a ballpark."

Urston glanced at the ceiling. "Anywhere from ten thousand to hundreds of thousands, sir."

Anger flashed across the President's face. "Why so broad?"

"We're without comms. Without any means of

assessing on the ground. A military drone flew over the area, but due to the incoming tsunami, sir, we haven't been able to do much more."

"There have to be scenarios written up for this. Some general ideas. I can't believe we're this unprepared."

Urston nodded in agreement. "There are, sir."

The President stared at him like he wanted to stab him with his signature pen. "And what do they say?"

"As you may be aware, sir, no area in the impact zone had a seismic code appropriate for a magnitude 9.0 earthquake until 1994. The vast majority of buildings in the area were built years, if not decades before then. Estimates out of Oregon put it at seventy-five percent."

"That are sound?"

Urston grimaced. "The opposite. According to our worst-case scenarios at FEMA, a million buildings have most likely collapsed or been compromised."

Someone seated at the table swore.

"How many are government?"

"Almost all government buildings will be affected." Urston paused. "And three thousand schools, sir. But that's not the worst of it." Urston paused again. "Fifteen percent of Seattle is built on liquefiable land, sir."

"What?" The President's tone shifted from one of annoyance to one of disbelief as the horror set in.

"It's ground that starts behaving like a liquid in a quake, sir."

"I know what liquefaction means, Urston. I meant, how was that allowed to happen?"

Urston shrugged. "Not my purview, sir." He cleared

his throat and kept talking. "As a result of the liquefaction, we expect up to thirty thousand landslides of various proportions in the Seattle area alone."

"You've spoken a lot about Seattle." The Head of Homeland Security spoke for the first time. "What about Portland?"

Urston flipped a page in his notes. "The majority of Oregon's liquid fuel flows through a six-mile section of Portland which we anticipate has suffered catastrophic damage. Combining pipe failures with damage to the electrical grid and natural gas terminals in the area, we could be looking at anything from fires to hazardous-material spills, to dam breaches."

Silence reigned around the table until the Chairman of the Joint Chiefs of Staff spoke up. "What were the warnings like? Are we looking at clogged roads, mass evacuations?"

"No, sir." Urston stared at his paper rather than meet the General's eyes. "Unlike Japan, we don't have an established early warning system that shuts down railways or power plants or opens elevators. The states on the West Coast did roll out a warning system in the last few years, but it's in the early stages, still. People may have been warned on their cell phones, but not until the ground started shaking in earnest."

"What a lot of good that did, I'm sure." The Vice President tossed his pen on the table and leaned back in a huff. "So how soon can we deploy to the area?"

Urston managed a conciliatory smile. He hadn't even

explained the worst of it. "Not until the tsunami retreats, sir."

Color drained from the Vice President's ruddy cheeks. "Tsunami?"

Urston nodded. "We expect—" he paused to glance at his watch, "the tsunami to be hitting momentarily."

"So, it's like a flood?"

"A massive, fast-moving wall of water, actually, sir. Our estimates put the tidal wave thirty feet high, at least."

"Will buildings withstand the force?"

"The ones still standing? Possibly. But the water will be moving unbelievably fast. No one will be able to swim or dodge. The ocean will swallow the land."

"So, your estimates of casualties—" The President began.

"Could go over one million when you consider the tsunami, sir. Six million people live in the combined metro areas of Seattle and Portland. If the water rises as quickly as it might, all those people will be trying to escape simultaneously."

Once more, the room lapsed into an uncomfortable silence. After a prolonged moment, Urston spoke again. "As soon as the water stabilizes, FEMA will be on the ground, bussing in food and water and coordinating with the National Guard of Washington and Oregon to triage medical care."

"What about search and rescue missions?" The Vice President, again.

"We're talking almost five hundred miles of coastline.

Thousands of square miles underwater, potentially for days. Obviously, National Guard and police forces will be combing the viable areas for survivors, but we'll have to wait for trained dive crews to recover many of the deceased."

The Chairman of the Joint Chiefs of Staff leaned toward the President and spoke in hushed tones. Urston couldn't make out the words, but he assumed it dealt with calling in active-duty military to assist. He waited until the conversation seemed to end before speaking. "FEMA is already in contact with our military liaison officers in the Army and Marine Corps. We're preparing to work with military bases in the area to stage supplies and possibly lend recovery assistance."

The President nodded in appreciation. "Once the rescue-missions are underway, what are the next steps?"

"Restoration. It will be slow. Estimates put electricity grid repair at three months."

"Three *months?*" The Vice President practically shouted.

Urston kept his voice even. "Maybe longer, actually. Think about all the flooded substations and downed power lines. All the destroyed transformers and collapsed buildings. Unlike a hurricane, where the area affected is relatively small, this is massive. It's not as easy as diverting or rerouting electricity from one area to another. The entire grid will essentially have to be rebuilt."

The President's eyes glazed over. The magnitude of the situation overwhelmed everyone who thought about it, Urston included. But they lacked the luxury of time to process and understand. Decisions needed to be made. Now.

He clicked to another slide where a set of bullet points outlined the major facets of FEMA's recovery efforts. "As I mentioned, we'll start with search and rescue, food, and water. After initial recovery efforts are undertaken, the electrical grid will have priority. Followed by the water system. Initial estimates put the ability to pipe safe drinking water to most residents of the affected area at a year, maybe more."

He glanced around the room. Gone were the cries of outrage and disbelief. In their place, a gathering of resigned men and women faced with a situation the magnitude of which none of them truly understood. No one made eye contact or even appeared as if they wanted to ask a question.

With a deep breath, Urston plowed ahead. "Tents will be set up at strategic locations throughout the impact zone. We plan to provide food and water for a minimum of three months. Busses will run continuously to transport most people out of the area and into neighboring towns where larger shelters will be established. Our goal is to essentially relocate most refugees within the first several weeks."

"*Refugees*." The word slipped from the President's lips, but he stared past Urston to the screen.

The Vice President leaned forward, drawing the room's attention away from the shattered President. "What about medical care? I'm assuming that's high priority as well?"

Urston nodded, grateful for the interruption. "It is, but we'll be needing to import most of that as well. Most local hospitals will be damaged, many completely destroyed. It will take years to bring medical capacity back to what it was before."

"But eventually, with concerted effort, it's possible, right? We can rebuild Seattle and Portland, at least. If not the small towns in between?"

Urston thought it over. "Everywhere except the inundation zone."

"The what?" The President cradled his head in his hand, staring at the desk as he asked the question.

"From the shoreline, inland, about twenty miles, we'll have what's termed the inundation zone. It's basically ground zero. Everything there will be destroyed. The coastline will be forever changed. For people who lived or worked in those areas, it will take years traversing the court system to become any semblance of whole. And their properties? They'll probably be beneath the ocean water forever."

The President held up his hand. "All right. I don't think any of us need to hear any more." He straightened his posture and tugged on the lapels of his suit jacket. "I'm declaring a major disaster right now. Let's provide assistance to individuals and households—I'm talking disaster unemployment, legal services, SNAP, anything and everything we can do for these... refugees."

He turned to the Chairman of the Joint Chiefs. "Then I want the Army Corps of Engineers out there rebuilding roads and bridges and working on the water

supply. Let's get all the military support we can muster—
I don't care if we're stepping on State government toes—
our men and women in uniform can help."

The Chairman nodded in agreement.

"Everything from distributing necessities, to running
shelters, to search and rescue. We can't let our people—
our *citizens*—die out there because they're trapped or
without food or water." He thumped the table. "This
might be the worst national disaster our country has ever
faced, but we won't throw up our hands. We'll do our
best to save as many people as we can."

The President's impromptu speech buoyed everyone
in the room. Even Urston puffed his chest out in
anticipation. He waited until the President turned his
way. "If that's all, sir—"

"Yes, of course. I'm sure you're needed in a million
places."

Urston nodded his thanks and strode from the room,
phone already to his ear. With the full support of the
Federal government, he hurried back to his office and the
overwhelming job before him.

"We're almost there, Pamela. Come on. You've got this."

Daphne clutched Pamela's waist, encouraging her to keep moving as she gently guided her down the aisles of parked vehicles. Her left hip screamed in protest with every step, Pamela's weight wreaking havoc on her joints.

"Which car is it?"

"That one, right there." Pamela pointed straight ahead as she gritted her teeth in pain. "It's that maroon Jeep Grand Cherokee."

Daphne inhaled. It was only another fifty feet or so. They'd already managed to escape the office and half stumble, half scoot down the stairs, but limping down the ramp of the parking garage meant Daphne was Pamela's only source of support. No handrail, nothing. Daphne took another step, but her knee threatened to buckle as Pamela shifted more weight toward her. She winced.

"I'm sorry, can you just—" With her free arm, Daphne reached for the trunk of the first car in the row, a low-slung sedan, and leaned against it. Pamela huffed herself onto the bumper and the entire rear of the vehicle lowered a few inches.

Daphne sucked in a breath. "I need a minute, that's all."

"It's okay. I know I'm heavy." Pamela dabbed at the thick sheen of sweat coating her forehead. Her chest heaved from exertion, blouse billowing up and down with every labored breath. "Thanks for helping me."

"Of course. I wasn't going to leave you on your own." Daphne stared down the ramp, past the Jeep, toward the exit. Cracks lined the concrete piers and a few cars suffered damage from falling debris, but the deck appeared sound. No heaps of rubble or collapsed ramps. At least not that she could see.

She sucked in a breath. Fifty feet, and then a vehicle. They could make it another fifty feet. Each step they took bridged the gap a little nearer. She shoved off the sedan with a smile. "At least the garage is still intact. We may have a real shot at getting out of here."

Pamela nodded as she prepared to push herself up to stand. "We have to count our blessings, yes."

Daphne resumed her spot beneath the larger woman's armpit and braced her one leg as she hoisted Pamela upright. "We survived a monster quake. We can survive the walk to the car."

One step at a time, they closed the distance, finally reaching the dust-coated Grand Cherokee as Daphne's back spasmed in protest.

Pamela pressed the unlock button on her key fob and

the vehicle's lights blinked on and the locks released. She held the keys out to Daphne. "Thank you for driving."

Daphne took the keys and waited as Pamela half-fell into the passenger seat before hurrying around to the driver's side. She pressed the start button and the vehicle revved to life. It took all her self control not to cry out in relief. They were going to get out of the city. They were going to be all right.

She shifted into reverse, backing out of the parking spot before driving down the ramp. More debris greeted them on the lower levels, chunks of concrete huddled together like still lifes at the corners of each ramp. But Daphne navigated them all without issue, bumping over the metal grate dividing the deck from the road, before braking to scan the street.

Daylight streamed across the dash and Daphne forced all the air from her lungs for the first time since the quake. She stared out at the scene before her in a combination of shock and disbelief.

Dust hung suspended in the light, drawn up from the ground and hurtled skyward. Buildings leaned over the road like menacing ogres, stone and brick shifted into haphazard stair steps before tumbling off the sides into heaps. What used to be an apartment building, now resembled more of a landfill than anything, siding and drywall and windows piled on top of each other like so much trash. One section survived relatively intact, towering over the collapsed remains.

A fridge teetered on the edge of what used to be a kitchen, door open, contents scattered. A dining chair lay on its side, back dangling two stories above the ground. From the now open air of a fourth story apartment, a man stood, hand covering his mouth.

Devastation. Everywhere.

A few people milled about on the street, but not as many as she expected. She heard what sounded like shouts and turned toward the noise. A man waved his arms, high over his head, as if in warning. Daphne squinted. Was he yelling?

She rolled down the window.

His words were still garbled nonsense.

"Do you hear that?"

Daphne squinted as if that would help her hear. "I can't make it out."

"No, not the guy. The noise. It sounds like a crowd cheering or... maybe running water. I don't know."

Daphne cocked her head, listening. Now that Pamela mentioned it, she *did* hear it. Low and unrelenting, almost like a wind tunnel. She glanced back down the road and froze. The man was gone, but from far away, down past the way he came, she saw it.

Not a mass of cheering marchers. Not some artificial wind turbine. But water. A massive wall of water.

"Oh my God." The words tumbled from her lips and she cranked the wheel.

"What?" Pamela pulled down the passenger mirror and peered behind them as Daphne jammed the accelerator. "What is it? What's wrong?"

"W-water," Daphne stammered. "Behind us."

"What?" Pamela twisted in her seat, attempting to

see out the back window. "I don't... I don't see... Oh, God."

Daphne clamped her lips shut and gripped the steering wheel with both hands as she accelerated down the street.

Water poured down the street behind them, filling the side mirror with horror as it swallowed up parked cars and debris. A bus tipped on its side, overcome by the wave. The water pushed it, lifting it into the air an impossibly high, ten, twenty, then thirty feet, before swallowing it like a gaping maw of a colossal whale.

It weaved through the handful of still-standing buildings, in broken windows, out second stories. As the water reached a building no more than a hundred feet behind them, the entire structure listed hard, the force of the wave toppling the unsecure stone and concrete. It fell in slow-motion, story-by-story, landing with a splash.

They were going to die. There was no way to outrun it. Nowhere to hide.

Pamela said nothing. She stared, transfixed at the devastation unfolding behind them, digging her nails into the seat back.

"How far away is it?" Daphne nudged her with an elbow. "Can you tell?"

"What?" Pamela fixed her with a wild stare. Her lips hung open, pink tongue hovering in the dark cavern of her mouth.

"The water! How far away is it?"

Pamela turned back to the rear window. "Not far enough."

"Is this thing four-wheel drive?"

"Y-yes."

"Good." Daphne slammed the gas pedal to the floor. The vehicle bounced over cracks and divots and hunks of torn apart asphalt. Daphne dodged a spill of debris in one lane and the remnants of a car crash in the other.

A beleaguered woman with a streak of dirt or dried blood running down her face stepped onto the road and Daphne cranked the wheel.

Pamela screamed.

They missed the woman by a foot. Maybe two.

"Can you slow down?" Fear coated Pamela's question, but Daphne ignored it.

She blared the horn instead, honking over and over as they neared an intersection. Without a moment's hesitation, she blasted through it.

Pamela clutched the sides of her seat. "You could have killed someone!"

"If we don't get out of here, the water is going to kill us," Daphne protested. "It's gaining."

She glanced in the rear view to confirm, even though she already knew the truth. It wasn't a flood or a breached levee. It was a tidal wave. A tsunami pushed in from the coast. She didn't know why she hadn't thought of it. Why reality hadn't forced its way in minutes ago.

They were in Bellevue, east of Seattle. It meant the coast, downtown, the heart of Seattle itself was already underwater. Thousands of people were dead, crushed by the force of the wave, or drowned beneath its depths.

Daphne wasn't going to be a statistic. Not after

surviving the quake. She pushed the pedal down and rocketed through another intersection. Everything blurred beside her. The debris, the damaged cars, the intermittent people. Pamela screamed and squeezed her eyes shut as Daphne took a corner too fast. The Jeep tipped, running on two wheels as it turned.

As she cranked the wheel back to neutral, the Grand Cherokee landed hard on the ground, bouncing from the impact. Pamala reached for the dash, bracing herself against it as they sped on.

"Can you see it?' Daphne cast a quick glance at her passenger. "Have we put any distance between us and the wave?"

"How would I know? You're throwing me around like I'm a sack of potatoes. If you would only slow—"

Daphne struck the side mirror of a car parked parallel on the side of the road, overcorrected, and almost plowed into a disheveled man standing on the sidewalk across the street. Her throat was in her chest.

"You almost ran over that guy!"

"I know, I didn't mean to." Daphne eased off the gas, her knuckles stark-white gripping the steering wheel. Beside her, Pamela began to hyperventilate. *One, one, two, two.* Short, sharp breaths. Her whole body bounced up and down.

"It's going to be okay." Daphne didn't mean it. "Please tell me we've gained some space."

Pamela dared a cautious glance out her side mirror. She reached for her neck. Covered her collarbone. "It's closer. How is that possible?"

Daphne swerved onto the sidewalk to avoid a stalled car in the middle of an intersection. She clipped the side of a trashcan and it flew up and over the Jeep before bouncing off the windshield and onto the road. A crack blossomed across the glass.

"You're going to have to pay for that."

"Not high on my priority list at the moment, Pam." Daphne squinted at the road ahead. Cars clustered at the next intersection, clogging the road and blocking their path. She eased her foot off the gas. Was there even a way to get through? She tugged at her lip with her teeth. They didn't have time to stop and think.

They didn't have time to do anything. She risked a glance behind them. So close. The water gained, unrelenting in its ferocity, but was it shallower? She couldn't tell.

Daphne turned to her left and right. There had to be a solution. Her heart lodged itself in her throat and she hesitated, the car drifting to a stop.

"What are you doing? The water is gaining on us!" Pamela practically yelled. "We've got to move."

Now she wanted Daphne to move. If they ever made it out of this, Daphne was giving this woman a piece of her mind. She held up a hand when the stenographer opened her mouth again. "We need to get to higher ground."

She swung her head, scanning the left and then the right. A little blue sign with a white P hung half a block ahead. "There!" She pointed at it before accelerating again.

"Where? The road is blocked, just like you said."

Daphne sped to the parking deck entrance. As she turned toward the ramp, Pamela threw her hands up in disbelief. "Are you crazy? Why would we go inside another parking garage?"

Daphne angled the Jeep through the narrow entrance and up the first ramp. "Because it's the only choice we have. If we can reach the top before the water, we might survive."

Pamela's eyes darted back to the street, but she said nothing. Daphne hit the gas, weaving up ramp after ramp after ramp until they crested the deck. It had to be four floors at least, maybe more. Would it be enough? She hoped so.

Daphne shoved the vehicle in park before throwing open the door.

"What are you doing?" Pamela leaned over, peering out the opening.

"We need to get as high as possible. This might not be enough." She scanned the deck. They were almost the only vehicle. Definitely the tallest. "We should climb on top." She hurried around to the passenger side and threw open Pamela's door.

"I can't climb anything with this ankle," Pamela complained.

"You're going to have to," Daphne urged. "You made it all the way from the conference room to the garage back at the law office."

Pamela's jaw tightened in defiance, her eyes glinting with frustration. Daphne felt the frustration too. It coiled around her spine and dripped down her back, mixed with sweat and fear.

But she couldn't give up. She had a daughter to live for, a daughter whom she desperately wanted to kiss and hug and apologize to for all the mistakes she'd made.

If she ever got the chance to see Mika again, she'd make sure the girl knew how much she was loved and wanted. She would put her first above all else. But she would have to survive to have that chance.

"Come on, Pamela." Daphne reached for the stenographer's hand.

Pamela shook her head adamantly and crossed her arms stubbornly over her chest. "I'm not going up there. I'm still trying to recover from the mini heart attack you gave me. You aren't a race car driver, you know."

Daphne ignored the digs. "Pamela, we've got to get to the highest ground possible. The water doesn't care who we are or how we drive. It's going to cover everything. I don't want to die here. If you don't want to drown, come with me."

Pamela's eyes were swollen and her nose red. She'd been through the wringer. Daphne held out a hand. She refused.

"Fine." Daphne sucked in a breath. "Stay there if you want, but I'm climbing onto the roof."

Daphne hopped on the hood of the car and shimmied to the top. Once she was in position, she carefully stood up and looked all around at the streets below, searching for the water.

Clint shoved open his door and stumbled from the cab. Neither Jack nor Jason followed. He spun on his heel and his expression hardened. "You coming or not?"

Jason shook his head. "No way. We're almost to safety. I'm not risking my life for a bunch of strangers."

Clint turned toward the Strait, although the water was obscured by buildings. He had to make a decision. "We don't have much time, but we might be able to get some people out of here. It's worth a shot. We can't just run and do nothing."

Jack cast his eyes at the road for a long moment before shoving open the door to the truck. "You're right."

Jason followed Clint's gaze, fear glazing his eyes. "But what if we don't make it back in time? We could get swept away."

Clint exhaled and his shoulders sagged. "I know you're scared, but if we don't try, then we're just as guilty as the wave. We can do this. We can help."

Jack grabbed Clint by the arm. "Ignore him. He can help or not. Doesn't change what we do." He tugged Clint away from the truck with one hand, cupping the other around his mouth. "You have to evacuate!" He shouted at the crowd. "Move to higher ground!"

The gaggle of people turned but didn't break apart. They didn't understand. Clint pointed toward the Strait. "Water's coming. We're going to flood!"

An older woman waved at the building next to them —a doctor's office that had collapsed during the earthquake. "We're safer out here. That building almost killed us."

Clint tried again. "It's a huge, massive wave. If you stay here, you'll drown."

The woman shook her head. "And go where, exactly? We're safe outside."

"No, you're wrong. It's coming. You have to get out of here." He held out a hand and almost pleaded. "Please, we've got to hurry." He raised his voice. "We've all got to hurry!"

A prim, younger woman decked out in athletic gear jogged over. "What makes you think—"

"We've seen it." Clint cut her off.

"A wave?"

"Yes. And the Strait—it's receded first. That's what happens before a tsunami. All the water the ocean sucked out is crashing back. We'll be smothered. Swept away."

Her eyes widened and she froze for a moment, horror settling across her features like the dust from crushed debris. "A tsunami? When?"

"Now."

She turned back toward the shop and the gathered people. "Let's move! Everyone to higher ground. We're going to flood!"

Finally, the crowd began to disperse. Clint exhaled in relief. At least these people had a chance. He sucked in a breath, steadied his feet. Only... That rumble. It wasn't another earthquake. It was water. A massive wall of water.

The buildings blocked the view, but the ground told the truth. It was coming. *Right now.*

"Everyone, run! Head toward the mountains!" Clint screamed and made giant circle motions with his arms like a pair of twin windmills. Jack did the same across the street, shouting at everyone to run.

It was all they could do. If they stayed any longer... He shook the thought away and hurried to the truck, whistling at Jack as he ran. He jerked open the door and jumped inside. "Jack! Let's go!"

Jason still crouched in the back of the pickup bed, face slack with terror. He didn't make eye contact as Clint hopped behind the wheel.

"Come on! What are you waiting for?" Clint banged on the truck door with the heel of his palm. Jack picked up the pace, yanking the passenger door open as someone behind them began to scream.

Clint shifted into gear and bumped off the curb, honking as he picked up speed.

Jack twisted around to stare out the rear window. "The water! I see it!"

Clint risked a glance in the rear view. White froth sloshed and rolled down the street, cascading over shop windows and parked cars. The sheer force uprooted a redwood and ripped it from the ground like a giant plucking a blade of grass. It hurtled through the waves, impaling a store window. Clint punched the gas.

"We need more distance." Jack, ever the pragmatic voice of reason.

"No kidding." Clint hit the brakes, narrowly avoiding a man darting across the street in front of him. The truck fishtailed and Jason slid across the bed. *No time. We have no time.* Clint ground his teeth together and punched the gas. The vehicle surged forward again.

He drove past a woman standing stock still, transfixed by the sight. His heart constricted and his foot eased off the gas. *Maybe...*

"It's gaining, man. We can't stop."

Clint glanced at the mirror again. Jack was right. The water surged across the road, inky fingers stretching into every crevice and gap collecting debris like costume jewelry. It swirled toward them. This was it. No more attempts at saving neighbors and strangers. He had to survive for his daughter. He had to save her.

He stomped on the brake and turned off the main drag onto an empty residential side street running parallel to the shoreline. Waves crested no more than a hundred feet away, lashing houses, topping roofs, consuming everything in its path.

The sun glinted off the cresting wave in a blinding flash, making it look almost like an image from a dream.

The muted roar of water played like a soundtrack outside the truck and the vibration shook harder than the engine. Debris littered the leading edge; chunks of siding, broken trees, a mangled car. The force of the wave hurled a twisted hunk of metal so high into the air it seemed to hang in the sky for a moment before crashing back down.

The smell of salt water and fear filled the air.

They were witness to the undeniable power of nature, weather, and the earth. Of something bigger than themselves. It was horrifying and beautiful and on another day, in another time, Clint could have stared at it forever. But right now, he needed to flee. He hit the horn, loud and fast, again and again, hoping beyond hope no one was foolish enough to stay inside their houses.

Two houses ahead, a woman emerged, pink curlers tucked beneath a canted shower cap, nightgown torn along the bottom edge. A bruise discolored her left cheek. She'd survived the earthquake, but not without damage. He pointed toward the water as he slowed. "You've got to run. Now!"

She turned, brow crinkling in confusion, before her eyes widened in shock and awe. Clint didn't wait. He punched the gas. Jack turned around, watching as they sped away.

After a moment, he turned back around, somber and crumpled.

"Did she run?"

"Not fast enough."

Clint shoved it down—the sadness, the grief, the ferocity of the wave. All of it. He pressed his lips together and forced a scratchy swallow. Images of his daughter filled his mind: bracing as the ground shook beneath her feet, pack on her back, forest all around. She was safe from the water that high up in the mountains. But did she survive the quake?

What about Daphne? She worked in a high rise. If it wasn't leveled, she was about to be consumed.

At the next street, he slammed the brakes and cranked the wheel, making another hard turn out of the residential areas and towards Olympic National Park. Toward his daughter.

Jack tugged on his sleeve. "You okay?"

Would any of them ever be okay again? Clint grunted his response.

"Road's clear. We should make it."

Clint nodded and jerked his head back over his shoulder. "Jason, you still breathing?"

"I'm here," Jason croaked.

"Good." Clint focused on the road ahead as they sped up. They were almost there. Almost home free. Just a... bit longer. He forced himself not to think about everything they left behind. He could only focus on Mika. On finding her alive. He would worry then.

A car appeared down the street, tires screeching against pavement, barreling toward them with reckless abandon. It swerved, taking out a telephone pole, clipping it like it was nothing more than an obstacle in its path. The vehicle careened down the middle of the road, headed straight for them.

Clint gasped and gripped the wheel, yanking hard to

the right to avoid a collision. He struggled to maintain control. Jason screamed in the bed behind him. The car side-swiped them, impact jarring their bodies so hard Clint and Jack careened to the right and the driver's side window shattered. A face pressed into the car's windshield —a woman screaming as she slammed into their truck. She blinked at Clint, mouth open, eyes wide as she slid across her windshield. She dropped into the front seat before slamming onto the dash. Her head bounced off the steering wheel and her body crumpled forward.

The car veered left but he'd lost sight of it already. He sucked in a breath to calm his racing heart. Jack sat up, rubbing his temple where he'd slammed against the window. Was Jason... Clint turned, fearing the worst. But the man appeared alive, cowering in a ball in the truck bed, head down between his knees.

"You all right?" Clint called.

Jason's voice came back wobbly and raw. "I think I pissed myself."

"Wouldn't be the first time," Jack offered.

Clint turned back around. "Hold on." He eased the truck forward again, glancing from one side of the street to the other. The coast was clear. He snorted to himself. Actually, the coast was anything but clear. At the moment, it was buried under the force of more water than they could comprehend. He drove south, gaining in elevation each block away from the Strait they drove until at last, Jack relaxed beside him.

"I think we're high enough."

Clint slowed and turned around. Sure enough, the water appeared to have reached its end point, white froth licking at the street fifty feet below. He eased the truck into the parking lot of a small community garden and killed the engine. They had survived. But so many hadn't been so lucky. He hoped his daughter fared better than the thousands of residents of Port Angeles who'd just been swept away.

CHAPTER SEVENTEEN
MIKA

"Come on, Hamp. I know it's hard." Mika hoisted Hampton up higher and took another step. "It's just a little farther."

"Mm-hmm." Hampton stumbled and Mika fought to keep her upright. "My f-f-feeeeet are numbbbbb. 'N my fingerssssss are alllll tin-tin-tingly."

Mika clamped her jaw tight and kept going, tearing through the forest understory, and trampling the ferns. On a normal hike, she would take care, avoiding damage to any plant life. But now? With her best friend barely coherent and unable to stand without assistance? It took every ounce of inner strength not to give up and sag to the ground.

But the sun was setting and sooner rather than later they would be in the dark, on their own, with no shelter. She shoved the panic down and kept going, sights set on a rocky outcrop where she hoped they could tuck in for the night. Something poked her through the thin layer of hiking pants and she shifted Hampton's weight.

"W-wh-why are there t-t-two of youuuuuu?" Hampton almost giggled as she swatted at the air.

"It's just me. Same old Mika. Only one as far as I know." Mika tried to smile, but it came out in a grimace. How hard had Hampton hit her head in the crash? She wished she knew more about concussions.

In sixth grade, one of the boys in her class took a baseball to the head and was on a strict concussion protocol for months—staying home from school, no bright lights, no sudden movements. He couldn't even do homework for the first week. Doctors said his brain needed total and complete rest.

Was that Hampton's problem? Was Mika taxing her too hard when she should be lying down and taking it easy?

Mika hauled her friend out of the bushes and ferns and over to a large hunk of rock. Vertical striations ran the length of the rise and Mika nestled Hampton down beside the smoothest section. With a ragged exhale she slid the cooler and both backpacks off her shoulders before collapsing beside her.

Sweat slicked down Mika's back and she forced herself to slow her breathing. Hauling all the gear and half of Hampton's weight took its toll. She closed her eyes for a few minutes and exhaustion tugged at her, pulling her down toward sleep. But she couldn't risk it. Not yet. Not with Hampton so...

She turned to her friend. Hampton held one hand

out, turning it back and forth as she squinted. Mika leaned closer. "Is your hand okay? Did you hurt it somehow?"

"I t-t-ried to p-pick up a leaf. It's sllllllipppppery."

Mika frowned. There was nothing slippery in the vicinity, just a trampled-on branch with a few crunchy leaves clinging to the bark. "You mean these?" She plucked one and it crumbled in her fingers.

Hampton nodded, but the movement must have hurt because she cried out and reached for her head.

"Shh. It's okay." Mika rubbed her friend's shoulder. "Maybe you should take it easy. Close your eyes for a little while."

Hampton tried to respond, but the words came out garbled and thick.

Mika glanced around at the ground for something, anything, to distract them both. "Here. I'll go through these packs. See what we have."

She dragged the first one forward, a tan rucksack she believed belonged to a troop leader. "I bet those ladies stashed some candy in here, I just know it." She smiled at Hampton, but her friend didn't respond. Mika unclasped the buckle and pulled the top of the pack wide.

She set aside the wrinkled collection of maps she'd grabbed from the glove box and shoved inside before digging around to find what remained. "A flashlight, very practical." She held it up before setting it on the ground between them. "A backpacking first aid kit. Fantastic." She waggled it, too, before moving on. "Rolled up raincoat, a change of clothes. Soccer slides." She checked the sizes. Ms. Rogers, for sure.

Hampton grunted beside her and Mika took it as a good sign. She kept digging through the pack, pulling out everything from folded bandanas and spare wool socks to a dog eared paperback. "Ah-ha! I knew it!" At the bottom of the pack, stuffed into a small pouch, was a handful of Hershey kisses. She held one out to Hampton. "Here, I know you're not a huge chocolate fan, but I think in this case indulging is a must."

Mika waited as Hampton struggled to pluck the candy off her open palm. She watched with trepidation while her best friend picked at the foil wrapper, trying and failing to tear it off. "Here, let me help." Mika unrolled the wrapper and handed the little hunk of chocolate back to Hampton. The other girl took it and brought it up to her lips, but she didn't bite.

"Don't you want it?"

"I—I'm soooo tired. Can I sa-save it?"

Mika smiled. "Of course. You just lay back and rest and I'll take a look at these maps. See if I can plot a route home."

She reached for the maps, discarding the irrelevant ones, and settled on a trail map of the area. She unfolded it before spreading it out across her lap. Resisting the urge to snuggle next to Hampton and point out every landmark, she instead satisfied herself with checking on her friend every minute or so, confirming her chest rose and fell in regular rhythm while she rested. She remembered that now sleep was recommended for concussions—that boy in her class had to nap multiple times a day. So, she didn't worry when Hampton slipped into sleep. It was good for her. What she needed.

And it gave Mika a chance to study. She focused all her attention on the map, struggling to place them on its topographic ridge lines. She glanced up at the darkening sky. Sunset was coming, fast. If only she knew where they were when the van crashed. But she hadn't been paying attention. She scanned the area, hoping to find something, anything, that looked familiar. But it was all the same—lush greenery, tall trees, rocky outcrops. Nothing to signify elevation or location or even proximity to town. They could be one mile or ten miles away and Mika didn't have a clue.

Tears welled in her eyes, but she brushed them away with the back of her hand. She couldn't afford to have a meltdown now. Her father would be coming, of that, she was sure. All she had to do was keep herself and Hampton alive until then.

She turned back to the map, tracing her finger from the beginning of the National Park towards the interior, attempting to distinguish the main road from the litany of trails. It appeared as if Ms. Rogers had marked their campsite with a bit of yellow highlight. Mika chewed on her lip as she studied it. They had to be at least halfway there, right?

Glancing up again, she tried to gain her bearings. Assuming they were halfway, then maybe, just maybe, the dotted black line curving up the ridge was the road.

And if so, Mika guessed they were somewhere within a zone on the map about fifteen miles away from town.

The more she studied the map, the more sure she became. She remembered the hook in the road just before the tremors started. And how Ms. Chalmers mentioned a scenic overlook not that far away. If she was right, and they could find the road, it might only take a day to reach town. Two if they took it slow. She glanced up, excitement lighting up her face as she turned toward Hampton.

"Hamp, wake up. I think I know where we are. It's not so bad. We sleep here tonight and in the morning—" She cut herself off. Hampton wasn't waking up. She nudged her friend's shoulder. "Hamp?"

Nothing.

She nudged harder and Hampton slumped over, sliding into a heap against the rock. Fear bloomed in Mika's chest. She shoved the map aside and crouched in front of her friend. "Hampton, please. It's Mika. Can you wake up for me?" Scared of shaking her in case it made the concussion worse, Mika tapped Hampton's hands and then her legs before pinching her bare arm.

Still nothing. Mika swallowed and leaned closer, jabbing two fingers into Hampton's neck to find a pulse. Relief flooded quick and hot when the steady beat pressed against the pads of her fingers. Hampton was alive.

Maybe the concussion was even worse than Mika feared. Maybe rest was the best thing for her. Mika twisted her fingers around each other as she stared at

Hampton's slack face. It had to just be a concussion, nothing more. She forced her runaway imagination to slow, banishing all thoughts of catastrophic injuries she couldn't name.

Hampton would be fine. She needed rest and recuperation, that was all. Mika was exhausted herself and she hadn't been thrown from the van. It made perfect sense when she laid it all out. Especially when she refused to consider any alternatives.

With a deep breath, Mika settled herself down beside Hampton and pulled her friend closer to rest on her shoulder. If she couldn't wake Hampton up, then she would at least sit beside her. Keep her company while she dosed.

After plucking the map off the ground, Mika spread it back out on her lap, intending to peruse it while Hampton slept.

Water. Everywhere. Clint's eyes fixed on the horizon as the tsunami crested in the distance. The water was a murky brown, churning with debris swept up in its current. A fridge rolled in the waves. A smashed car slid to a stop at the edge of the road, pushed forward by the force. A body hung limply over the ruined roofline of a flooded home.

The parking lot of the community garden remained clear, but froth clung to the low-slung library across the street. How many people up and down the coast just died? A thousand? Tens of thousands? More?

"Are you okay?" Jack called out.

"Is anyone?" Clint couldn't tear his gaze away.

"No, them." Jack nudged his shoulder and Clint turned. A bedraggled group of survivors edged around the library. A man carried a toddler, her blonde hair falling over his shoulder. A woman held the hand of a little boy. Dried blood clung to her forehead and the boy limped, obviously injured.

"Survivors." Clint's breath caught in his throat.

"Are you all right?" Jack spoke louder and the man jerked his head in their direction.

His face was streaked with dirt and sweat, eyes red-rimmed and haunted. Shock and chaos and the threat of death aged him, although he must have been a decade younger than Clint. The woman stepped forward, her voice shaking, "Our house is flooded. Four, five feet of water inside. We barely got out."

The little girl winced and wriggled in the man's arms. "Daddy, I'm cold."

"I know you are, baby." He hoisted her a bit higher in his arms. "Do any of you have a blanket we could use? Or a jacket?"

Clint strode back to the truck and flipped the seat, rummaging through the small storage space in the back. He pulled out a wool blanket he kept for emergencies and held it out to the man. "Take it."

"We can give it back as soon as—"

Clint waved him off. "No need. Are you injured? None of us are doctors, but I've got a small first aid kit."

The woman spoke again. "I think we're okay. Billy here twisted his ankle running, but..." She trailed off.

Face pale with shock, the little boy clung to his mother, silent and still.

"He's okay?"

She swallowed back a sob. "He tried to get our cat."

Billy tugged on his mother's pant leg. "*My* cat."

"Any luck?"

The woman shook her head. "No sign of poor Fluffy. One minute, we were playing board games in the living room, all enjoying the day off, and the next thing I knew, the floor started to shake. It was small at first, you know? But it kept going on and on. The pictures fell off the wall, the mirror toppled over with a crash. Dishes bounced out of the cabinets."

"We made it to the hallway, thinking we'd be safe there. But then a crack formed along the wall and every shake pulled it farther apart and smashed it back together. The floor rose and fell, I swear more than a foot." The man shook his head in disbelief. "I thought it was the worst few minutes of our lives. We were so thankful when the shaking stopped. We thought it was over."

"So did we," Clint offered. It wasn't much consolation, but it was true. None of them thought about the potential for a tsunami, even though most people who lived in the area knew the odds. But in the moment, after you've just survived something so terrible and vicious, well, Clint didn't give much thought to anything. If he hadn't seen the Strait, understood what the receding waves meant...

He glanced at Jack. They'd be dead.

"When the water came, we—" the woman faltered. "We weren't prepared. All of a sudden it washed in over the broken front window, into the entry, the dining room, lapping at our feet in the hall. We had what," she glanced at her husband, "seconds before it was knee high?"

"By the time we made it out the back door, the couch was floating. I've never..." The man ran out of words.

"We ran this way as fast as we could." The woman managed a grim smile. "Bella isn't the quickest, so—"

"Am too," the little girl protested, rising off her father's shoulder to scowl at her mom. "But up is hard."

Clint smiled at her. With any luck, she'd only have vague memories of this day as she grew up. "But you all made it. That's the important thing." He glanced at the truck where Jason still sat in the back, refusing to take part in the conversation. Refusing to do anything except keep himself together. At least he hadn't completely fallen apart. Not yet, anyway.

"Is there somewhere we can take you? Somewhere not flooded?"

The man focused somewhere over Clint's shoulder, searching for answers. "Maybe the elementary? Franklin, you know it?"

Clint nodded. It's where Mika went all those years ago. "It's on a rise, should be dry."

"I'm guessing it'll be a rally point, right? Maybe a shelter?" The woman offered.

Jack spoke for the first time in a while. "It's a warming shelter in the cold months, so that's a good guess."

Clint motioned toward the truck. "You're welcome to climb in the back. I can ask Jason to cram in the front with us." He turned toward the vehicle, but Jason was already moving, hoisting a leg over the side as the family approached. He settled in the front, taking up as little space as possible and Clint and Jack crammed in on either side.

Clint managed to shut the driver's door as the man eased his daughter over the side of the pickup and into the bed. The woman reached out, steadying her daughter as her husband handed the blanket over. She wrapped her daughter in it before pulling her close.

Once they were all situated, Clint turned to Jason. "You okay?"

Jason nodded. "I can't stop thinking about all the people." His voice was low and shaky. "All the people we just lost."

"Hopefully this family's the rule, not the exception." Clint started the engine and eased out of the parking lot.

The road leading to the elementary school was littered with debris. A single-story home stood alone on the nearest corner, surrounded by tall pine trees, half toppled, branches and needles strewn about the lawn. At first glance, the home appeared unscathed, but as they neared, scattered bricks from the broken chimney clogged the road. Part of the foundation gaped and crumbled, revealing hints of the basement below. Was any house in Port Angeles intact and livable?

Clint eased around the bricks and other debris and headed away from the flood water and the closest east-west road to the school. He made it only another block before a downed tree completely blocked their path.

With a frustrated sigh, he turned the truck around and headed back toward the water.

"What are you doing?"

"Peabody Creek runs right through this area, remember? If we can't cross on Lauridsen, we've got to circle back to Eighth."

"But that's where we were. When the wave came." Jason looked like he might throw up.

"We don't have a choice." Clint kept driving, inching around debris and clumps of mud and bracken washed up with the now receding water. Cars and trucks sat smashed against one another where the wave propelled them like pinballs. Trees leaned drunkenly from their roots, snapped like toothpicks by the force. In some places, houses stood mostly together, but others looked as if they'd been torn apart, leaving only splintered wood and shattered glass behind.

After another twenty minutes of stops and starts and backtracks, they finally reached the elementary school. Thanks to the three-day weekend, they were spared the chaos of several hundred terrified children waiting for their parents, but the parking lot appeared congested all the same. People milled about, some wrapped in blankets, others wet from the ankles, or knees, or waist. One man held a towel to his forehead, blood dribbling down his cheek.

Clint pulled the truck up on the side of the road and shifted into park. "We can walk up from here. Stay out of the parking lot in case anyone is trying to stage a relief effort." He flashed a tight smile at Jason and Jack before hopping out of the truck.

The family did the same, woman helping her daughter over the edge and into her father's waiting arms. He nodded at Clint. "Thanks for the ride. And the blanket."

"I'd say anytime, but hopefully nothing like this ever happens again."

The man smiled in agreement and Clint walked on, bypassing a small gathering of locals who appeared scared, but unharmed. It didn't take long to find someone he knew.

He clapped an older man on the back. "Bill, how are you?"

The man turned around and smiled. "Clint, thank God. Did everyone make it out of the Port?"

"Think so." Clint ran a hand over the back of his head, rubbing up and down as he thought it over. "Not sure about the marina or the businesses down the way. But the Port offices, yeah. All accounted for."

Bill nodded. "Good. Good." Principal of Franklin Elementary, Bill Patrice was one of those men you used to say came from good stock. A Port Angeles family for multiple generations, his father was a logger, his grandfather before him. Bill was a kinder, gentler soul and preferred the education of little ones. But it didn't make him soft. No, he was the best principal the town ever had. It made sense he was here, overseeing recovery efforts.

"How is it going?"

Bill pointed up the hill. "We're setting up a triage center in the gymnasium. All injuries will be seen to there. The school nurse, Nancy, you remember? Same as when your little girl was here, I believe. She was here catching up on paperwork for the state, so she's got a good head start."

"What about food, shelter?"

"Cafeteria is going to go operational this afternoon. Hot meals as long as we have supplies. Don't know how many people to expect, so can't really say how long that'll be." Bill stepped closer as the wind lifted his white hair. "I've heard the first five blocks of town were swept away. Nothing left but water."

Clint reeled. If that were true, his house was gone. As were hundreds of others. "What about the medical centers by the coast?"

"I'm guessing there's nothing left. What the quake didn't tear apart, the water swallowed." Bill glanced at the ground. "We might have lost half the town."

Ten thousand people? Was that possible? Clint stared out at the blue sky beginning to pale in the late afternoon. "Mika's on a camping trip with her scout troop. In the Park."

Bill whistled low. "At least you know she didn't drown."

"But that doesn't mean she's alive."

"You headed there?"

Clint nodded. "If the house is gone, it doesn't matter if I stop by to check, now does it?"

Bill managed a chuckle. "Guess it doesn't." He gave

Clint's upper arm a squeeze. "You get out of here. Go find that daughter of yours. We'll still be here when you get back."

Clint nodded his thanks. After making eye contact with Jack and nodding toward the truck, he took off at a lope. Now that he'd dropped everyone off somewhere safe, he was off to find his daughter.

CHAPTER NINETEEN
DAPHNE

The water barreled into the town, over the streets, lifting cars, toppling streetlights. It swelled beneath them, edging up the side of the ruined building across the street. Bubbling and gurgling below them. She turned to the stenographer who sat on the edge of the passenger seat, legs splayed out, heels digging into the painted stripe of the parking spot.

"Pamela, you've got to get up here. The water, it's—" she searched for the word. "Relentless. I'm afraid—"

"We're four stories off the ground. And how many miles inland? There's no way the ocean will surge this high. We're fine."

Daphne worried the chipped edge of a painted nail between her teeth. "You can't see it, but I can."

"Then where is it, exactly?"

Water lapped at the exterior of the deck. Daphne stretched tall, rising on the bare balls of her feet, but it was no use. She turned toward the ramp and squinted into the dark. Was it coming?

She sagged back down to her heels. "It's multiple stories high, I can see that much."

Pamela snorted out a reply and turned away from the open door, heaving herself fully onto the seat.

Daphne resisted the urge to argue and lowered into a seated position on the hood. It flexed beneath her weight but held her fine. She sat there, hands on her knees, as her blood rocketed through her veins and her fingers trembled. This was worse than the quake in a way. The expectation. The suspense.

She closed her eyes and listened. Beneath the jagged breath and steady beat of her heart, she heard it. A slow roar like a sound machine or TV back when you could tune in static.

As she opened her eyes, she sucked in a deep breath. Mixed with the smell of old oil and gas and concrete was something new. Something earthy and moist. Musky, even.

Flood water.

Rising on shaky legs she peered over the edge of the deck before turning back to the ramp. Was that—?

"Pamela?" Her voice came out as wobbly as her legs. "Pamela? You need to get up here."

The other woman didn't respond. Daphne fell to her knees and leaned over, peering into the vehicle. Pamela leaned back in the passenger seat, earbuds in her ears. She was listening to music? Now?

Daphne slammed her fist on the roof of the Jeep, once, twice, three times, and Pamela's eyes popped open.

"What the heck? Can't you see I'm resting?"

"The water. It's here." Daphne jabbed her index finger in the direction of the ramp. You've got to get up here."

Pamela made a show of putting her earbuds away and shoving her phone in her purse. Daphne glanced at the ramp. She gasped. How could it be coming that fast?

What used to be the faintest hint of water was now a steady flood. It inched up the ramp, dark froth in front, followed by muddy waves. Daphne twisted around on the roof in a panic. What if she wasn't high enough? What if it came for her? Could she swim her way off the deck and to safety?

Would the current be strong this far from the ocean? Like a riptide or worse? She shoved the thoughts away and leaned back over, searching for Pamela. "We're running out of time. Please, Pamela. Let me help you."

"It's not going to swallow up the car, Daphne. Besides, as soon as I haul myself up there, the whole roof is liable to cave in. If you haven't noticed, we're not in the same weight class, hon."

"It's worth a try." Daphne held out her hand. "Please."

Pamela stared for a long moment at the water as it lapped at the tires of the car closest to the ramp. "Let me pull some things out of the back."

Daphne waited, forcing herself not to announce every time the water reached a new landmark: the wheel well of the other car, the bottom of the windows, the roof. Pamela didn't seem to do well when faced with a sense of urgency. But every inch the water crept closer, Daphne struggled to stay quiet. If the other woman didn't crawl up there soon, it would be too late.

When the water tickled the closest parking stripe, she cleared her throat. "You about done, Pam? I think now's a good time."

"I still think you're blowing it out of proportion." Her voice came out muffled by the roof. "It's going to recede any minute now."

"Look around you," Daphne responded in an urgent voice. "It's going to fill the car soon. You need to get up here."

"And what happens when the water goes over the car's roof?" Pamela emerged from the vehicle and stared up at Daphne, defiance in her eyes.

She had a point. Daphne's eyes darted around at the water now creeping up the sides of the tires. There was no escaping it. She had no idea how to answer Pamela's question, but at least the roof was higher ground than the seats of the car.

"Please, Pamela. Humor me."

"Fine. Just give me one second." Pamela hoisted herself back into the passenger seat, one leg jutting out as she leaned over to reach for something. A garbled scream rose from inside the Jeep a moment later.

Daphne rushed to the edge of the roof, fingers splayed across the maroon paint as she leaned over. Water flowed into the cab, flooding out the front and back seats. Pamela's blouse floated in the murky brown waves.

"Pamela!" Daphne cried out as she scrambled to her knees and stuck a hand down toward the other woman.

Pamela stared up in shock. "The water is freezing. I didn't expect—It's moving so fast. I—I can't feel the lower half of my body."

"Give me your hand," Daphne urged, reaching for Pamela's arm.

Pamela linked her fingers to Daphne's and tried to lift herself, but the water was like a funnel, suctioning around her, holding her down.

"My leg—"

"Shove the pain aside and pull yourself up," Daphne commanded. "Come on. You've got this."

Daphne strained against the force of the current, pulling on Pamela's arm with all her might. The woman didn't budge. She tried again, sweat breaking out across her shoulder blades as she braced one palm on the roof and rose into a low squat. Using her legs, she pulled.

It wasn't enough.

The water rose higher and higher, inching up Pamela's torso to her collarbone. She fought to keep her chin above it.

"Can you get out? Get out and swim?"

"Maybe." Pamela sobbed, her features tortured.

Tears pricked Daphne's eyes in response. There had to be something she could do. Something to save the woman. "Come on. Just go with the current. You can tread water. Maybe make it to one of the other vehicles. Climb aboard.

Pamela nodded. Tears mixed with the flood water as it lapped across her cheeks. Daphne gave the woman's hand one more squeeze before letting go. It took a few tries, with Pamela rocking forward and back as the water washed over her face, but at last, she emerged from the vehicle.

Relief flooded Daphne, but it was short-lived. As soon as she was free, the current swept Pamela away, carrying her across the parking deck. Daphne screamed.

"Pam! Pam, just keep swimming. Keep treading water!"

A garbled wail carried across the water. Pamela flailed, arms jutting out before disappearing only to pierce the water and wave about. She wasn't treading water. She was panicking.

Drowning.

Daphne called out again and again, trying to give instructions, encouragement. Anything. But it was no use. She watched in horror as the woman's head dipped below the water. She popped up once, twice, but on the third time, she was gone.

"Pamela?" Daphne cried as she slid to her knees on the roof of the car, her eyes searching the water for any sign of the woman. After countless minutes searching, Daphne sagged in defeat. Pamela was gone.

As the shock wore off, a sob rose in Daphne's chest and for once, she didn't shove it down. She embraced it, wallowing in the heaving, stomach twisting grief. Her ribs ached, her throat burned and the tears flowed unending down her face.

Was everyone in the building dead? What about the countless other buildings all around Seattle and Bellevue? She clambered back up and stood on the roof, searching for any sign of life.

She inched forward and her toes met the ocean. She recoiled from the shock. Cold and thick, full of debris and mud and murk. The water wafted over the roof, not high enough to cover, but enough to soak her feet and keep her from sitting down.

There was nowhere else to go. Nowhere else safe from the water. She was stranded.

The sun eased lower and lower in the sky and at some point, Daphne noticed the water had stopped its relentless pursuit. The roof of the Jeep was wet, but not submerged, so at last, she eased down to sit. She sat in a daze, body and soul numb, mind a blank canvas.

At last, the sun disappeared behind the damaged horizon, turning burnt orange as it set behind a building only half its original glory, the top floors now resting in a heap beneath the ocean surge. It was exquisite, almost painfully beautiful, and Daphne closed her eyes.

She couldn't bear to look at the pastel pinks and sherbet orange hues, the stalks of lavender painted across the sky. She didn't deserve to see something so spectacular. To take part in the splendor of nature after what she'd just endured. After what she'd failed to do. Guilt scratched her throat and twisted her stomach, and she stared out at the now dark water, searching for any sign of Pamela.

As dusk gave way to night, and the moon took up residence high and full above her, she spotted the woman. Or the hulking, floating shape of her corpse, at any rate. She bobbed in the water like a floatie in a suburban pool. Daphne turned away.

Hunger rumbled in the tight knot of her stomach and Daphne longed for any scrap of comfort. A blanket, a cup of coffee, a text from her daughter. The thought of Mika brought a fresh wave of tears, but Daphne wiped them away. This was all her fault. She was sitting here, alone on top of a dead woman's car because of what?

Is this really what I wanted? To be all alone in this huge city of chaos and grief? The two people I care most about in the world hundreds of miles away?

She had it all, and she destroyed it. They had fallen into routine in Port Angeles. Her the homemaker, Clint the breadwinner. And with Mika growing up so fast... Daphne had been adrift. Unmoored. And over the years, they had drifted apart. Stopped talking and sharing. Started living these independent lives like silos, like partners in the business of raising their child. Not husband and wife.

She'd thought that meant they were no good for each other anymore. That she needed to move on, chase those dreams she'd had so long ago. But maybe... Maybe they'd both just stopped trying.

In the past year how many times had they even spoken? Once? Twice? Now it was just impersonal texts, schedule coordination. She'd been lonely in Port Angeles, but she was lonely in Bellevue, too. Leaving Clint and Mika changed nothing. It only took a disaster and a flood and a car up to its neck in flood water for her to see it.

She stared up at the moon, thoughts consumed with Mika and Clint. That they were safe. Unharmed. She had faith in her ex. He was an excellent, hands-on father. He would protect Mika. They were alive, she felt it deep in her soul.

With her eyes on the sky, she fixed an image in her head of the pair at home, watching the moon from the serenity of their backyard. Clint's arm slung over Mika's shoulder as they laughed and reminisced and cried. After a deep breath, she dropped her head and clasped her hands together. They would be okay. They had to be. Daphne began to pray.

Mika sucked in a sharp breath and jolted upright as if lighting had ripped down her spine. Her skin was clammy and drenched in a cold sweat. Her hoodie clung to her back, damp from perspiration.

It all came rushing back. The quake. The crash. Hampton. She reached out and cold rock lined the space behind her, not the snugness of her bed. It wasn't a nightmare. It was real life.

She fumbled in front of her as she blinked the darkness back, attempting to focus in the moonlight. Her fingers flitted over the map and a random assortment of items from the backpack she'd been rummaging through. *I must have fallen asleep.*

"Hampton? Hamp are you awake?"

No response.

Mika searched with her fingers until she found the small flashlight. She cranked the handle until the flashlight's glow burned steady and the little alcove tucked beside the rocks illuminated.

She found Hampton slumped over, a limp arm laying slack across her lap. "Hamp, wake up." Mika reached for her best friend, grabbing the girl's bare arm. It was colder than the night air.

No. No, this isn't happening.

"Hampton!" Mika screamed as she hovered in front of her friend, willing her to rise. "Come on, stop fooling around." Mika's voice caught in her throat, the words dissolving as tears spilled over her lower lashes.

She grabbed Hampton by the shoulders and pulled her close. The girl's head lolled to the side, hanging at an unnatural angle like a puppet left to dangle by marionette strings. *So cold.* Why was she so cold?

Cradling Hampton in her arms, Mika reached around to feel her neck, shoving the tangled mass of curls away, searching the hollows of her flesh for a pulse. Over and over she moved her fingers, jabbing deep into Hampton's cold skin, praying for the faintest flutter.

Tears spilled down her cheeks and landed hot in Hampton's hair. "Please wake up. Please, Hamp. I need you. Please don't leave me all alone out here. Please..." She trailed off, unable to contain her pain and heartache.

Mika hugged Hampton's body closer, pressing their hearts together, squeezing hard. Hampton loved bear hugs. She would laugh and squeal and pretend to escape, until they both collapsed in a fit of giggles. But now she just hung there. Sagging. Empty.

A shell of her former self.

How long had she slept while the life slowly drained from Hampton's body? How long had it taken her best friend to die? Had she woken up? Called for Mika?

Guilt wormed its way into Mika's heart and lodged there. Guilt for falling asleep, for not checking on Hampton every few minutes, for not knowing how to treat her when she was obviously injured. She'd been so focused on finding a way off the mountain, on contacting her dad, that she hadn't really considered Hampton's injuries. Hadn't really focused on her friend.

Pain rubbed raw across the back of Mika's throat and she wilted into Hampton's limp form. How many times had Hampton tried to weasel out of the trip? How many times had Mika insisted she would love it? She barked out a tortured laugh.

If it weren't for her insistence, Hampton would be home right now, snug on the couch between her parents watching some rom com on the Hallmark Channel. She stilled.

After a moment, she eased Hampton away and leaned her gently up against the rock. For the first time, she thought about more than the mountain. More than Olympic National Park. If the earthquake caused landslides and tremors so strong the road ripped apart, what did it do to Port Angeles? Seattle?

We're Hampton's parents even alive? What about Mika's? She tried to shut off the spiraling thoughts, but they wouldn't retreat no matter how much she concentrated. Stuck five thousand feet above sea level in a National Park with no cell phone, Mika had no idea what was waiting for her when she finally made it back down.

The death toll might be unimaginable. Port Angeles might be heaps of rubble. Seattle and Bellevue might be gone. Imaginary images paraded through her mind. Collapsed buildings. Buckled streets. Dead bodies.

It was too much for Mika to bear. The idea of her parents being dead, of her being orphaned—well—it was simply incomprehensible.

Mika blinked up through blurry tears to stare at the moon. Full and round and unobscured, it shone down on the forest, lighting up the ferns and rocks with a soft, silvery glow. She closed her eyes and listened to the sounds all around her.

A gentle rustle in the understory a few feet away. A swish-swish of the wind through the trees. Not everything was destroyed. Life went on in myriad ways all around her. With a hard sniff, Mika straightened up. She dug the ends of her palms into her eye sockets and rubbed away the last of her tears.

She scooted next to Hampton's body and snuggled against it before resting her head on Hampton's chest and closing her eyes. "Remember when you got gum stuck in your hair and we tried to get it out with peanut butter?"

Mika laughed as she talked to the air, no one around to reminisce with her. "Mrs. Dougherty in English was convinced someone was eating in class the next day. Kept saying she smelled a pb&j."

She pretended like Hampton was listening, recalling other memories and laugh-crying at each one. The gaping hole in her heart eased a bit with each memory, and eventually she swallowed down the rest of her grief.

Despair snaked and coiled around her spine, tucking itself in for the long haul, but Mika tried her best to ignore it. She was still alive, not seriously injured, and she could survive out there. Hampton would be so angry if she simply curled up in a ball and let her sadness overtake her. She could hear her now, cajoling her with promises of hot chocolate and fluffy blankets if she would only get off this stupid mountain.

Mika thought about her family. Her mom in Bellevue and her dad in Port Angeles. Her father was a survivor. He knew what to do in a crisis and was more experienced in the outdoors than Mika. If anyone could find her, he would. He loved her and wouldn't rest until she was found, safe and sound.

After a few minutes, Mika stood and brushed the dirt from her jeans. She wiped her damp cheeks and her wet eyelashes with the sleeve of her sweatshirt, cleared her throat, and took a deep breath to compose herself.

If Port Angeles was gone, if Seattle was a heap of collapsed concrete and steel, then no one would be coming to recover Hampton's body. No one would be searching for survivors in the middle of the park. Mika couldn't bear the thought of animals finding Hampton's body and feasting. And she couldn't carry her friend's body more than a few feet before collapsing.

She stared down at her friend's lifeless body. It wasn't ideal, and if she thought about it long enough, she would chicken out. But she owed Hampton a proper burial. Her friend deserved to rest in peace, not decay out there in the forest, human fodder for the creatures of the day and night.

Mika retrieved the small hand shovel she'd found in Ms. Rogers's backpack and used the flashlight to canvas the area around them, trying to pick out a level spot of ground. Somewhere with a decent view.

She found a spot a few paces away and dropped to her knees. After staring at the ground for a moment, she opened the shovel to its full length and began to dig. It took an eternity. By the time the grave was deep enough to lay Hampton in and give her at least a modicum of cover, Mika was exhausted. Every muscle ached. Her neck barely moved. Dirt lined the crevices beneath her nails.

An owl hooted in the distance and Mika managed a tight smile. *At least I'm not the only one out here.* Mika cleaned her hands with a towel, not wanting to use up any of the drinking water. Her fingers were still a little grimy, but it would have to do for now. She trudged the few steps back to the makeshift camp and knelt beside Hampton.

Pain and loss threatened to rupture inside her, but she held herself together. "Okay, Hamp." Her voice came out in a shaky whisper. "It's time to go, now. I promise, you will never, ever have to go camping again. I hope you are up there dancing and putting on makeup and using that curling iron you loved way too much. It can't ever fry your hair again, so go crazy."

A sob shook her to her core and she rocked back on

her heels. "I miss you so much." With a deep breath, she steadied herself before reaching out and wrapping her hands around Hampton's wrists. "This isn't going to be the most glamorous of moments, but I think you'll understand."

Mika braced against the weight and crouched to use more of her leg muscles as she dragged Hampton's body toward the grave. A few steps and she stopped to breathe. A few steps more. At last, she reached the makeshift grave and gently nudged her friend down the embankment.

With gentle hands, Mika repositioned Hampton's body, straightening her legs, tucking her hair behind her ear. She didn't have a bouquet of roses or a fancy blanket to drape over her best friend, so she simply reached down and hugged her one last time.

She cried quietly into Hampton's curls, whispering words of love and sadness and guilt and apology. When her body gave up, refusing to make any more tears, Mika forced herself to move. She climbed out of the grave and one scoop at a time, she shoveled the dirt over her best friend.

It took longer than expected to escape Port Angeles and the destruction. Before he even reached his truck, Mika's third grade teacher asked him to help cart her wheelchair-bound mother to the elementary school from their house a few blocks away. When he finished, the band leader asked Clint to haul the snacks and water out of the band closet and to the cafeteria.

He hated to refuse, but every minute stretched out the time his daughter was without him. He called her cell again. This time it didn't even cut to voicemail. It was just dead air. Nothing. No way to hear her voice, even in the form of a message.

He pulled up the phone locator app as he sat in the driver's seat of his vehicle. The little dial whirred and whirred. Cell towers around the area must be damaged. The app was probably overloaded. People in Seattle and Portland trying to find their loved ones when they couldn't place a call.

Horrifying images paraded through his mind. A car crash. An explosion. A landslide. Mika burning alive, or buried under a landslide, or drowning in a river of water streaming down the street. Mika pinned under a tree, gargling, choking on her own blood as the life slowly left her fear-widened eyes. He shut his eyes, screwed his palms tight against his eyelids. Imaginary torture would get him nowhere.

He shifted the truck into drive as someone waved their arms to flag him down. Without a second glance in the man's direction, Clint pulled out of the lot. Enough helping. Enough delays. He needed to find his daughter.

Taking the main road out of Port Angeles, Clint avoided the worst of the debris and the residents of the town, huddled in bewildered clusters on the broken sidewalks and ravaged front yards. He entered Olympic National Park and pulled into the parking lot for the visitor's center. Part natural history museum, part ranger station, the visitors center was the entry point to the entire region.

He parked in front, noting the handful of cars. A crack snaked through the concrete steps leading to the front doors and glass littered the ground where two large windows shattered. But the structure appeared sound. He made his way to the door and tugged it open.

A solitary ranger busied himself behind the main information counter, rummaging through cabinets and loading what appeared to be a substantial hiking pack. He glanced up when the door closed with a thud. "Park is closed. Too much damage to assess."

Clint flashed a grim smile. "I'm looking for my daughter."

The man didn't look up from his task. "Is she a ranger?"

"Girl Scout. Her troop left Port Angeles this morning, heading into the park to camp and hike. I was hoping someone here would know exactly where they were headed."

The ranger stilled, a first aid kit in his hand. "How many girls?"

Clint approached the counter. "Twelve, I think. And two adults." He was close enough to read the man's badge. Brad. Head Ranger. Younger than Clint by five years at least, he was ruddy complected and stout. Built for the outdoors. "Did they check in here?"

Brad shook his head. "I'm not sure. I had the afternoon shift. Margaret was on in the morning, but she left to patrol right before the quake." He swallowed. "Haven't seen her since." He put the first aid kit down and strode to the other end of the counter. "If they checked in, there might be a record on paper, although most of that's digital now."

He scratched the back of his neck. "Computers are down, I'm afraid."

Clint waited, hands shoved in his pockets to keep from fidgeting. He knew it was a long shot, coming here. But he had to try. If only he'd asked Mika for more details. Pushed harder to find out the specifics. But he hadn't wanted to seem overbearing. Overprotective.

Brad pulled a tattered binder onto the desk and

flipped through it, shaking his head as he finished a section. "There's nothing here." He shoved the binder aside and disappeared in a crouch. His voice came muffled from below. "I don't see anything." He stood up with a conciliatory smile. "I'm sorry. Most of our campsites are on the honor system. You sign up on the cork board and put your money in the slot. Campers don't have to stop if they don't need to."

Clint nodded. He'd feared as much. "If you were taking a gaggle of teenage girls up here, where would you stay?"

The ranger thought it over for a moment. "Heart O' The Hills, maybe. It's got a full bathroom." He walked out from behind the counter and motioned at a map on the wall. He pointed out their current location and the campground. It wasn't far.

"And if that isn't it?'"

Brad exhaled long and slow. "Honestly? They could be anywhere. Hurricane Ridge is quiet this time of year. They might have headed that way. Duncan is probably on shift today at that station. You could ask him. He's been a ranger here longer than I've been alive. If anyone knows the good spots, it's him."

Hurricane Ridge was a recreation area popular in the winter months for skiing. Clint had taken Mika there countless times when it snowed. He thought about the elevation and the drive. It had to be at least fifteen miles away. "Is it accessible?"

"No idea." Brad shook his head. "The quake activity's been intense. I've gotten reports from a handful of rangers on the radios about landslides. I was loading up to head out on patrol just now."

Clint stared at the map. Campsites dotted the park, many accessible only via foot trails. It was a lot of ground to cover. "Do you know if things have settled down? The landslides, I mean."

"No clue. Sorry."

He exhaled. Apart from the two places Brad mentioned, Clint had no leads. He didn't even know if the roads were passable. But what choice did he have? The truck could make it over buckled roads and minor washouts from collapsed hillsides. But a major landslide? He'd deal with it when he got there, he supposed. The alternative wasn't an option. He glanced around the place. "Mind if I load up on a few things?"

Brad hesitated. "I'm not really supposed to be open. I mean—"

Clint leveled him with a look. "If my house didn't collapse in the quake, it's underwater. My wife is somewhere in Seattle, probably buried under rubble, and my only child is stuck somewhere on this mountain. I've got a quarter tank of gas, no food, no water, and no supplies. I think you can spare a few minutes."

The ranger nodded weakly. "Go ahead."

Clint hurried, grabbing water bottles, energy bars, a first aid kit, an overpriced backpack to stuff it all in, and a few more odds and ends. He wished he had his own gear, but that was all long gone, he assumed.

Brad glanced at the cash register. "Power's out. I can't ring you up."

Clint reached for his wallet and opened it up. He pulled out a few twenty-dollar bills. It's not enough, but it's what I have." He held it out.

"You know what? Don't worry about it." Brad held up his hands like he was shoving the air in front of him. "Under the circumstances, I don't think anyone will care."

Clint nodded his thanks. "You don't by any chance have a gas station around here, do you?"

Brad shook his head. "Not here. But Hurricane Ridge has a small tank used for Park vehicles. If Duncan's on staff, you might be in luck."

"Appreciate it." Clint swung the now loaded pack onto his shoulder and headed out of the ranger station. He didn't have a clue where his daughter might be, but that didn't deter him. He was on a mission, and he wouldn't leave the park until he found her.

CHAPTER TWENTY-TWO
CLINT

Clint followed the road signs to the Heart O' the Hills campground and eased the truck past the closed ranger station and into the first loop of camping spots. He pulled over at the large bulletin board set up with do-it-yourself reservations and hopped out, scanning the cards for anything recognizable. He didn't see the troop name, or the scout leaders listed anywhere.

He hopped back in the truck and eased it down the first loop until a fallen tree forced him to reverse. It had been tough going to even reach the camping area—with fallen trees and buckled roads and two landslides in his path. But he'd managed, barely. Now he was faced with the prospect of searching the campsites on foot. He glanced at the sky. Daylight was fading.

He hopped out of the truck and hesitated for a moment before making up his mind. If she were here and he left... No. Even if it burned precious daylight, he needed to be sure. Clint hurried on foot, jogging around the loop of campsites, not finding any evidence of the Girl Scouts. He clambered back in his truck and repeated the process on the other loops, checking the campground registration boards and driving or jogging around the loops to be sure.

No evidence of Mika. Not one bit. With a heavy heart he hurried back into his truck and drove back to the main road and on toward Hurricane Ridge. It took longer than he bargained for. At one point, he doubted his ability to continue, stymied by a two-foot diameter tree he couldn't hope to move. But his truck managed to crawl over the rocks flanking the road, one tire sticking in the loose soil for a moment.

He pulled up to the day lodge as the sun set behind the distant mountains. As he climbed out of the truck, he paused, a view open of the mountains all around. On any other day it would take his breath away. But he might as well have been staring at a blank wall. Mika filled his mind. Her whereabouts. Her safety.

Without a moment's delay, he hustled to the front of the lodge and took the steps two at a time. He pulled the door open and bells jingled above his head.

An older ranger with a smattering of gray hair stubbornly clinging to his scalp glanced up from a far corner of the room. He held a broom and a dust pan and appeared to be cleaning up the remnants of a broken window. "Welcome to Hurricane Ridge, although to be honest, I'm surprised anyone is stopping in."

Clint nodded in agreement. "I'm looking for my

daughter. She came this way on a Girl Scout camping trip this morning. I'm hoping you might have seen them."

The ranger pressed his lips together, thinking. "We had a few groups this morning. Have any more details?"

Hope bloomed in Clint's chest and he quickly relayed all he knew.

The ranger dashed his optimism. "I'm sorry, I don't remember a group like that. We had a couple families early, and then a small group, maybe three teenagers and a mom? I was hoping that might be your girl."

Clint rubbed the back of his neck. All this time and he wasn't any closer to Mika. The sun inched lower behind the mountains and he stepped forward to counteract the fading light. "Are you Duncan by any chance? Brad down at the visitor's center said you knew all the spots to camp. Might be able to point me in the right direction."

The man smiled. "That's my name, although Brad might be a bit optimistic on the campsite front. People aren't supposed to, but they do camp out in the woods, you know. Away from any designated spot."

"I don't think that's an issue with these girls. The troop leaders run a tight ship."

Duncan cocked his head, thinking it over. "In that case, I have a few ideas. Come over to the counter. I'll pull out a map."

He leaned the dustpan and broom against the wall and headed over to the information area. Clint waited as he spread a map over the counter and pulled out a pen. Duncan circled a spot on the map. "We're here." He made a handful of X's in the vicinity. "The popular trails leading out of Hurricane Ridge are here, here, and here. And each take you to some lovely hike-in camping areas. Did you check out Heart O' the Hills?"

Clint nodded. "No luck."

"Worth a shot. It's the easiest campsite up this way." He highlighted three more areas for Clint to explore. They were spread out, requiring miles of hiking between each one. How would he choose where to start? How would he ever find his daughter?

"If you were leading a group of twelve girls on a trip here, where would you camp?"

The ranger thought it over before pointing out an area on the map. "Here. There's some lovely views a mile or so in and the campsite is primitive, but clean."

Clint examined the area. He'd need to backtrack in the truck quite a ways and follow the road until the trail veered off. He glanced out the window. There was no way to make it before dark.

He rubbed his hand across his lips. "Any chance you can spare a bit of gas? If I've got to search all these areas, I'm going to run out before I make it through the first half."

Duncan appraised him long and hard, as if sizing up the type of man he was. At last, he nodded. "Sure thing. I'll have to take you to the shed. It's locked for security purposes."

Clint thanked him and headed out to the truck, following Duncan in his small ATV away from the lodge and to a service road. They puttered down the road a few hundred yards before Duncan pulled up next to a large shed. He motioned for Clint to approach. Clint waited as the other man unlocked the shed and swung the door wide. Inside, a single gas pump with manual controls, installed decades ago, sat beside a Park-owned 4x4.

He pulled the truck up and killed the engine. Duncan filled him up.

"Can I pay you for the gas?" Clint offered.

Duncan waved him off. "No need. It's not like the Federal Government will miss it, will they?"

"Suppose not." Clint glanced up as the sound of an engine filled his ears. A truck with a massive metal bumper splattered in mud, rumbled into the parking lot, idling in front of the lodge. He turned to Duncan. "You should probably get back."

Duncan eyed the other vehicle. "Looks like it."

Clint motioned toward the lodge. "I'll drive over. Wait until you're inside."

"Appreciate it." Duncan closed the shed and locked it before climbing back into the ATV and making his way to the rear entrance of the Lodge.

Clint waited, out of earshot of the other vehicle, until Duncan headed toward the stairs. "You all right? Want me to stay?"

Duncan glanced at the mystery vehicle again. "No need. If things get interesting, there's a rifle under the counter."

In the moment, Clint wasn't sure a rifle would be much of a deterrent. Duncan was what, sixty? Sixty-five? He might be fit for a man of that age, but he'd be no match for a kid in his twenties. Clint had seen enough videos of gas station employees attacked to know a rifle didn't ensure anyone's safety.

He lingered in the lot, unsure what to do. The truck still idled in front of the Lodge, occupants not leaving. Duncan disappeared inside. Maybe he would be okay. Maybe it was all in Clint's imagination. How many people were already up to no good a few hours after a natural disaster?

Too many, most likely. People who were desperate before, already living on the edge, were probably tipped over now. Any shred of morals out the window.

At last, he eased by the lifted truck, slowing as he left the parking lot. In the rear view, he watched the driver's side door open and a man climb out. The man pulled the hood of his sweatshirt up and hiked his jeans. Was that the glint of a gun in his waistband?

Clint was too far away, and it was too dark now to be sure. A pang of guilt hit him. He should go back and help Duncan, a man who'd been nothing but good to him. But then he thought of Mika. If things went south... If he got shot or worse... Who would find her? Who would save her?

With a heavy heart, he pushed down the accelerator and left the Lodge, Duncan, and the stranger behind.

He focused on the road and the map, driving with purpose to the first of the trailheads Duncan marked. He would hike these hills all night if he had to. He wasn't leaving the forest without his daughter.

As the Lodge slipped out of view, he swore he heard

what sounded like a shot. His foot eased off the accelerator, but he forced himself to keep driving.

Mika needs me. My daughter is in trouble. I can feel it.

He tightened his grip on the steering wheel. Every decision he made from here on out was for her.

CHAPTER TWENTY-THREE
MIKA

Mika stood, staring at the night sky full of countless stars. If she shoved everything out of her mind, she could almost pretend her entire world hadn't upended. She wasn't alone, on the side of a mountain, covered in dirt and sweat from burying her best friend.

But she was calmer now. Resigned.

A slow building of resolve had been forming deep within her. A grim determination to find a way out of the forest and back to civilization. Hampton wouldn't have wanted her to sit there, consumed in grief. She'd have wanted her to survive.

Mika walked back to where she'd left the meager items she'd managed to pull from the van: a cooler and two backpacks. She'd already inventoried Ms. Rogers's pack before Hampton... She shook her head to clear it. The cooler held bottles of warming water, sandwich fixings and what was supposed to be tonight's dinner—

hamburger patties and chopped potatoes ready for cooking over a fire.

With no energy to build a fire, the dinner food was useless. She forced herself to open the lunchmeat and cheese, rolling it up between her fingers and eating it like a burrito. Guilt rolled around in her chest, battering and bruising her insides as she chewed. If Hampton had been there, she'd be complaining about the smell of turkey on her fingers and how some black bear was sure to come upon them and devour them whole.

But her only company was the wind waving the ferns and the owls hooting in the distance. She finished the food and wiped her fingers on her pants before reaching for Hampton's pack. She'd held off on opening it, unable to face the last traces of her friend.

Now she didn't have a choice. If she was going to hike back to Port Angeles, she needed to consolidate. Only bring what was useful and what she could carry. With a deep breath, she unzipped the purple nylon and pulled the pack wide open. She cranked the flashlight she'd found in Ms. Rogers's pack—one of those small, battery-free ones with a crank to generate electricity—and peered inside.

Metal glinted off the light and Mika stared in disbelief. "Really, Hamp?" She pulled out the infamous curling iron. "You brought it anyway?"

Visions of Hampton holding up the curling iron in the middle of the woods, lamenting the frizz in her hair, brought a sob to Mika's throat. She sniffled and pinched her eyes shut for a moment. Tears threatened to overflow, but she willed them back, regaining control.

She grabbed her half-empty bottle of water and drank, coating her raw throat and easing the sting of unshed tears before turning once more to the pack. What followed was a parade down the things-not-to-bring checklist: a bottle of electric-blue nail polish, eyeshadow and mascara, a fashion magazine. A grief-filled laugh bubbled up inside and Mika slumped over the useless pack, crying over Hampton's choices and her loss.

She'd take Hampton and her backpack over food and shelter any day. But she couldn't will her friend back. Couldn't even will herself off the mountain. Mika sucked in a deep breath and shoved all of Hampton's things back inside the pack and zipped it up. Carefully, she leaned it against the boulder and took a moment.

The flashlight faded, finally flickering out. She sat in the darkness, contemplating her next move. It was too dark to see, let alone hike. And the crank flashlight only lasted a minute or two before fading out. Add in the body aches and fatigue from endless digging and Mika had no choice. She would have to camp out overnight and take off in the morning.

She reached into Ms. Rogers's bag and pulled out the tarp she'd found earlier. It wasn't much, but strung up between the rock she leaned against and the closest tree, it might keep her dry if it rained overnight. It was always a possibility in the area. She steeled herself and stood, fluffing the tarp to its full, unfolded length, before hoisting it over the largest boulder.

Using the crank flashlight to see, she scrambled on top of the rock and weighed the tarp down with handfuls of smaller rocks and debris before scrambling back down. Then using a rolled-up strip of paracord she found tucked in a side pocket of the pack, Mika pulled the tarp taut and secured it to the closest tree, a scrawny pine no bigger around than her wrist. It bent as she tied the cord, but it would spring back in the morning.

Out of breath and sweaty again, she pulled Ms. Rogers's lightweight sleeping bag from the pack and nestled herself into it, using the backpack as a pillow. It wasn't the best set up in the world, but it was better than nothing.

She closed her eyes and tried to sleep, but visions of the crash and the van and the dead bodies filled her mind. With a deep breath, she rolled over and tried again, but it was useless. Her mind refused to quiet, reliving the horror of the day over and over in slow motion. She sat up and grabbed the flashlight, cranking it once more to life.

The map was where she left it, sitting on top of a jumble of rocks to her left. She reached for it and once again spread it out in her lap. With a pen she found in Ms. Rogers's pack, she noted the road leading out of Port Angeles and into Olympic National Park and the highlighted campsite, once again narrowing her focus to an area fifteen to twenty miles away from town.

Now the only question, could she figure out exactly where she was?

She studied the trails, thinking hard about her prior trips into the forest. If only she'd paid more attention when her dad pointed things out. Instead, she'd always plastered her forehead to the passenger window and stared at the sheer expanse of green everywhere she looked. What did it matter what road they were on or where the campsite was located when her dad had it all under control?

Mika chewed on her lip, trying to remember. They'd sung how many songs before the earthquake? Five? Six? The van was loaded down and cruising pretty slowly once they gained in elevation, so that meant they were going, what, twenty-five, thirty miles an hour?

Memories of her math teacher explaining how practical applications of math skills were all around them filled her mind as she struggled through the calculations in her head. Using the mileage marker on the map as a guide, she drew little question marks on all the roads at the fifteen-mile point, noting where they might have crashed.

It wasn't perfect. A long way from it. But it was better than nothing. If she could head north, and maintain a descent as she hiked, she would have to reach a ranger station or a campsite at some point.

The hint of a plan calmed Mika and she stifled a yawn. She set the map and the pen to the side and snuggled back down into the sleeping bag. At first light, she'd pack up and be on the move.

Mika blinked her eyes open. The hint of dawn stretched across the horizon, lightening the forest from darkest black to desaturated gray. Pale yellow sky peeked from behind the trees and Mika eased out of the sleeping bag. Cool morning air greeted her and she shivered.

Time to move.

She shoved the remaining water bottles into Ms. Rogers's backpack, along with the tarp and everything else she thought she could use and forced herself to eat another wad of meat and cheese. With the ice melted and the temperature outside rising, bringing the cooler wouldn't be worth it. She'd risk food poisoning for sure.

Mika zipped up the backpack and glanced over her shoulder, pausing a moment as her gaze landed on the mound of fresh dirt. Hampton's grave. Her eyes watered, but she wiped them dry with the back of her hand and turned around, inhaling a heavy breath of mixed emotions.

"Love you, Hamp."

She picked her way through the ferns and foliage, mindful of where she placed her feet. A twisted ankle would only compound the danger. She found a gnarled, but strong stick a few feet long and picked it up, using it to lift the ferns and check for snakes and other critters.

The sun rose, warming the air and bringing the full radiance of the forest—the rich greens and browns—to life. She picked her way toward what she hoped was the direction of the road. It was slow going, navigating the quake's destruction, climbing over fallen trees, circling around sinkholes and loose soil. But she kept going, steadily working her way.

Hope filled her as she walked, lightening her load

and her steps, until a sound pricked her ears. She slowed. Turned around. Scanned the forest.

Funny. She could have sworn she heard something.

Mika shrugged it off and kept walking until a feeling lifted the hairs on her forearms. She turned around again. Still nothing. But this time she couldn't shake it. She was being followed.

Every noise made Mika flinch. Echoes of every breath buzzed in and out of her ears. Her heart galloped ahead.

Something or someone was watching her.

She turned around again. Still nothing. "Whoever you are, leave me the heck alone!" She shouted into the forest, willing the terror to vanish with the breeze.

It didn't work.

Mika turned back around and picked up the pace. She stumbled onto what looked like a trail and she took it, not caring whether it meandered to the road she so desperately needed or up the mountain. All she cared about was getting away from whatever was following behind her, whatever was keeping out of sight in the leaves.

A twig cracked and she whipped her head. Her eyes went wide. Her whole body froze mid-step.

It wasn't a person. It was a cat. A tan, lithe creature, it prowled thirty feet behind, giant claws digging into the earth. Mika swallowed. A mountain lion.

She'd never seen one alive, in person before. A stuffed one fake-prowled the visitors center at the park entrance, and she'd seen plenty of photos and videos of them as a kid, but in real life? As it stalked her like prey?

It was large but thin, ribs clearly visible. Was it starving? Is that why it chased her? If only she still had the cooler full of rotting meat.

She stared at the animal. It took another step closer. Its tail swished. She backed up. The mountain lion advanced.

Mika shouted at it. "Go away! I'm big and scary and I don't want you here!" She waved her arms.

The cat advanced.

She broke out into a backward run but the animal ran toward her, closing the distance to no more than twenty feet. It jumped and opened its mouth, half growling, half hissing. Panic welled up inside her.

"Go away!" She windmilled her arms. "Get!"

She scuttled back. The mountain lion advanced again. *This can't be happening.* She scanned the area for something, anything to use. The walking stick. She changed her grip and shoved the end of the twisted branch at the cat. It swiped its paw as it jumped a foot in the air, undeterred.

She shouted again but the cat ran at her, darting forward three or four steps until it skittered to a stop as she shouted even louder. "No! No! I'm not food for goodness sakes! Get away from me!"

They were fifteen feet apart.

Mika backed up, slowly this time, arms out in front of her, waving like crazy. All the time she kept talking, kept shouting at the animal to go, to leave her alone. Nothing was working. The cat flattened its ears and hissed, but Mika managed to put some distance between them. "Okay, it's okay. Just leave, please."

She kept walking backward. The cat yowled again, still following, still stalking.

Mika glanced behind her, checking on the trail. As soon as she turned her head, the cat charged, ears pinned to the back of its head, front paws out wide as it lunged. Mika screamed and hurled the walking stick in the cat's direction.

The animal stopped, kicking up dust on the trail. "Please, cat. Please. I don't know why you're interested, why you suddenly care about me, but I'm not a threat and I'm not food. Just leave me alone."

Mika was all turned around. She had no idea where the trail was taking her, whether it was headed north or south or some other way entirely. For all she knew, she could be walking in circles. But none of it mattered if the hungry beast trailing her attacked. She'd never survive. Not those claws. Not those teeth.

Mika bent down and grabbed a rock and threw it. The cat flinched as the rock sailed wide. She picked up another rock.

"Get away from me!" She threw the next rock and again it went wide.

The animal's tongue slid across its snout, pink and

gritty. A shiver jogged through Mika's bones. Panic stirred inside her. She fought the urge to run.

Again, she bent to grab a rock. This time, the animal advanced as she crouched, and Mika threw the rock in a blind panic. It landed with a thud in the dirt behind the mountain lion. Missed again.

The cat prowled closer. Mika licked her lips. How long had this dance been going on? How far had they walked? She canvased the ground for anything bigger she could launch at the cat to force it to flee. There was nothing.

With as much strength and determination as she could muster, she took another step back and then another. The cat followed. Half of her wanted to give up, to curl up into a ball and let the darn thing eat her. But she thought of her dad, somewhere out there looking for her, and of her friends now dead somewhere nearby, and it steeled her resolve.

She puffed out her chest, waved her arms. Screamed as loud as her lungs would allow. No words this time, just a primal, desperate wail.

The cat stopped and stared. Mika screamed again. The sound pierced the forest, painful even to her own ears. The cat's ears twitched. The muscles in its shoulders flexed.

Mika took a cautious step backward, her eyes still locked on the animal. Maybe this was it. Maybe it would leave her alone. She took a step backward.

The cat advanced.

Mika's stomach bottomed out. She fought a wave of

nausea. "Leave me alone," she cried in frustration. "Go away, please. I won't taste good. You don't want to eat me."

Her legs wobbled and she tripped on her own foot, stumbling as she half fell. Her hand landed on the ground and she scraped her palm on a rock bigger than her fist. She closed her fingers around it and tried to pick it up. It was heavy and lodged in the dirt.

With a tortured groan, she stopped and bent down, glancing at the cat as she worked to prise the rock from the earth. The cat swished its tail again but didn't attack.

Mika grunted with effort, finally dislodging the rock from the edge of the trail. "All right, you jerk. Let's see how you like this."

Mika hauled the rock up and over her head, bracing against the weight, and threw it as hard as she could. It sailed through the air and although the mountain lion swerved, the rock clipped the animal in the shoulder. It cried out in anguish and in a torrent of dust and howling, galloped away in the opposite direction.

Mika watched until the trees hid the cat from view. Hunched over, gasping for breath, she gripped her thighs hard above her knees. Her hands shook so badly, she balled them into fists to regain control. Never in her life had a wild animal given her such fright. She'd known mountain lions were in the area, along with a million other animals, but she'd always been told they stayed away from humans.

Maybe the earthquake scared this one into action, or maybe it was starving with babies to feed. Mika didn't know and didn't want to find out. She forced herself to stretch to her full height and sucked in a lungful of air. She stood in the silence of the forest, listening. As far as she could tell, she was alone. The mountain lion was gone.

She turned back to the trail, trying to gain her bearings. After a few agonizing minutes, she was forced to admit the truth. She was most definitely lost.

CHAPTER TWENTY-FIVE
DAPHNE

Daphne worked her jaw back and forth, attempting in vain to ease the soreness. All night, she'd inhabited a tortured pattern—a half hour clamping her jaw so tight her muscles spasmed, a half hour letting go until her teeth banged together so violently she thought she'd chip one.

Her hair hung damp and heavy on her back, soaking her blouse and turning her skin moist and clammy. Flood water turned her pants dark, collecting in the wrinkles at her hips and behind her knees. She'd tried to save Pamela and soaked herself in the process. And now, as the sun's faint glow colored the horizon, what did she have to show for it?

Damp clothes, empty stomach, and a chill running so deep she swore her bones ached from it. She'd curled up into a ball at some point, cradled on the roof of the SUV, body racked with tremors. But it hadn't done much good.

She was freezing and hungry, holding her breath for the onslaught of a caffeine-withdrawal headache sure to come.

The light cast a pale yellow shimmer across the murky-brown expanse of water. It still covered the parking deck, the street, the whole entire city as far as she knew. She'd kept hoping as the hours ticked by for some relief. Some sign of receding water. Some hope that she would be able to walk out of there.

But no such luck. The stinking soup lapped at the hood of the Jeep, wafting over the window trim to tease her every time she shifted and the roof flexed. She inched her feet away.

As the sun continued its silent march, illuminating the destruction all around her, Daphne uncurled her legs and forced herself to stand, straddling the roof, bare feet inching toward the edges to keep the metal from denting any more. Water, everywhere.

She squinted against the morning light. The building across the street, once seven or eight stories was now compressed to not much more than the parking deck. Water bobbed in the windows on the fourth floor, glass long gone thanks to the quake or the force of the tsunami. A file cabinet, contents disgorged and disintegrated like a drunk after too many beers, floated in the water, drawers open and barren.

Was anyone else out there trapped like she was? Hungry and cold and without means of escape. She dug a fist into the hollow where her stomach growled behind her ribs. There had to be survivors. People trapped in hotels and apartment buildings that survived the quake. Penthouse prisoners.

Maybe the water warmed overnight. Maybe it wasn't the frigid, hypothermia inducing ocean water it had been the day before. She risked a tentative toe in the water and recoiled as the cold seeped into her skin. Daphne was a decent swimmer, but not in ocean water this temperature. She wouldn't be able to last long. The ocean currents filtered down from the arctic, never reaching much above fifty degrees this time of year, if they reached that at all. Being this far inland did nothing to the temperature.

She stared out at the horizon, searching for the end of the flooding, the return of city, and a chance at survival. Was it another mile? Two? Would the water recede in a day? Five?

Daphne inhaled, long and slow, until her lungs were fit to burst. Then she screamed. The loudest, sharpest, most primal and animalistic scream she could muster. It wasn't pretty or ladylike or anything her dead boss would approve of. But none of that mattered now.

The last vestiges of her voice echoed through the destroyed street and she sagged back down onto the roof of the SUV. She pulled her legs toward her chest and wrapped her arms around her shins, resting her chin on her knees. She debated stripping down to her underwear and spreading her clothes out on the roof, but they probably wouldn't dry. She might, but it wouldn't do any good in the long run. At some point, she'd be wet again.

Visions of Mika filled her mind again. She yearned for her daughter, desperate to hold her in her arms and cry until she was all drained out with no tears left to give. She had to have faith her daughter was alive and safe. That Clint had found her up that mountainside and taken her somewhere warm and comforting. Somewhere they could eat and sleep and forget the horror of the past day.

She gripped the top of the roof with her toes, clenching and unclenching as she thought about Clint. Closing her eyes, she almost felt his strong arm wrapping around her shoulders, warming her damp body, comforting her. If she imagined hard enough, she could feel his lips on her forehead, kissing away her worry and doubt.

If she ever saw him again, she'd apologize. Explain how she'd confused growing apart with falling out of love. How they were better together than miles away from each other, living separate, lonely lives. There was a reason she'd never taken the step of hiring a divorce attorney. Why she'd never pushed for more than separation. That had to count for something.

She snuffed back a wave of emotion and listened to the eerie quiet, straining her ears to hear something—anything. Any signs of life or stirring out there. The silence was deafening. Unnerving and unnatural. Usually this part of town was filled to the brim with the sound of traffic and honking horns and thousands of people going about their lives.

Her tongue stuck to the roof of her mouth and she

peeled it off, desperate for a sip of water. A laugh slipped out and she brought her fingers to her lips. All this water —as far as she could see—and not a drop fit to drink. Even if it weren't salty, it was full of sludge and debris. Countless chemicals. Dead bodies.

She pressed her dry, cracked lips together and used the discomfort to focus. Someone would come, surely. On a boat, a helicopter, something. Her mind played out two likely scenarios.

One, she remained on the roof of the Jeep, refusing to leave, body damp and cold, exhausted from hunger and thirst. At some point, she'd give out. Fall asleep and succumb to hypothermia or dehydration. She'd simply never wake up. Her body would rot there on top of that vehicle until the water retreated and someone came to assess the damage. How long would it take? Weeks? Months. She might be bones by then, stripped clean by carrion birds and bleached by the sun.

Option two, the distant chop-chop of helicopter blades stirred her awake and she stood, groggy from sleep and hunger to find a rescue bird hovering in the sky. She would wave her arms, frantic with anticipation and a long white rope and stretcher with railings would lift her to safety.

She envisioned a warm blanket wrapped around her shivering, frigid body. A bottle of water hastily shoved against her palm. It was almost too much to bear. This hope. But Daphne kept it close, tugged the pretend blanket tighter around her shoulders, basked in the relief of rescue.

After a long moment, she opened her eyes and looked around. Stared long and hard at the endless expanse surrounding her. There was no way out, and right now, no one was coming. All she could do was wait and pray.

CHAPTER TWENTY-SIX
CLINT

Clint adjusted his sweaty palms on the steering wheel and glanced at the clock. 7:37 a.m. He'd been driving and walking and searching all night, but so far, no sign of his daughter or the rest of the Scouts. The map Duncan gave him wrinkled as he reached for it. So many crossed out Xs. So many empty campsites.

Anyone who'd been out on the mountain when the quake barreled through appeared long gone. Trash littered a few places, as if campers left in a hurry—too shook up to take care. Apart from the truck at Hurricane Ridge, Clint encountered no more people, alive or dead. It was as if the mountain simply swallowed them up. He took a deep breath and exhaled slowly.

There were only a few places left to search. He picked up his phone and opened the locator app, hoping this time would be different. The little wheel turned and turned and Clint let himself hope. But it timed out, just like all the other failed attempts.

He shoved the phone back in his pocket and tightened his grip on the steering wheel. His heart still beat like a snare drum in his chest, refusing to calm down. At this rate, he'd shave a few years off his life without even trying.

A split loomed in the road ahead and Clint slowed to a crawl. Asphalt buckled and cracked, rising like a mini mountain range in the middle of the road before collapsing on the edge into rocky bits mixed with debris. He stared out at the terrain lit by the early sun. Rivers of rock and dirt wove through the forest, burying undergrowth and uprooted trees.

He blinked. Landslides.

In the dark of night, he hadn't seen them; didn't know the state of the mountainside. A fresh wave of worry hit him and he eased the truck over to the shoulder of the road. Up ahead, the whole span of road disintegrated, impassible even with his four wheel drive.

If the Girl Scout troop made it this far, the mountain might have swallowed them whole. He shifted into park, grabbed the map, and climbed out of the truck. According to Duncan, two campsites lay beyond the destroyed road. One two miles to the west, another three miles to the east. He would have to hike to each one, traversing unstable ground and hoping his movements didn't trigger another slide.

After circling his location on the map, he folded it into a manageable shape and oriented himself with the morning sun. He grabbed the pack from the Visitor

Center, stuffed with the meager bit of remaining food and water, and set off, heading west.

It was slow going, traversing loose rocks and dirt. Clumps of mud obscured buried shrubs and destroyed trees and more than once his boot punched through what appeared to be solid ground and lodged in a thicket of broken branches. As he took another step, he slipped on a hidden rock and scraped his palm. He cursed beneath his breath.

If Mika was out there somewhere, she was mired in the same terrain, trapped in the remains of a mountain once lush and verdant. Would a passenger van survive a landslide? Maybe if they eased off the road and hunkered down somewhere sheltered. A rocky outcrop or a bit of valley.

His heart ached for his daughter and he pulled out his phone again, hoping for a miracle. Still nothing.

He pressed on, climbing in elevation step by painstaking step, hoping to clear the worst of the debris. Time dragged as the sun inched higher and higher in the sky and sweat pinned the middle of Clint's shirt to his back.

At last, he neared a small ridge line and crested the worst of the landslide. His feet found solid footing on a clear bit of rock and for the first time since leaving the truck, he stopped to catch his breath.

The mountain unfurled below him, aftermath of a massive landslide on display. Where trees used to cling to the incline, a large swath of dirt and rocks lay instead like a massive brown glacier stretching down the side of the mountain, ending in a giant dirt pool below.

Clint stared, awestruck by the magnitude of the devastation. *Is that—?* He frowned and put a hand up to shield his eyes from the morning sun. The outline of something blocky and large loomed a hundred feet below him, ravaged by fire and caked in black soot . It stood out in relief against the paler dirt around it.

Could it be? Acid bathed the back of Clint's throat as he stepped down into the loose fill around the rocks. He couldn't tell make or model, but the burned out shell was a passenger van, of that he had no doubt. *Please have it not be Mika's.*

He kept thinking about his daughter. How he'd seen no glimpse of her anywhere in the campsites on the mountain. Was that because they'd never made it? Because they were trapped in the landslide, van tipping over as the dirt and rocks overtook them, only to crash into the forest and ignite.

He picked up the pace, stumbling through bushes and past trees until the toe of his boot caught on a hidden root and he pitched forward, barely catching himself before his face slammed into a jagged rock. *Steady, man. Don't be stupid.*

Clint fought the urge to run, forcing himself to stay vigilant and slow down as he traversed the dangerous terrain. If he twisted an ankle or broke a leg now, he would never forgive himself. With his eyes focused on the ground in front of him, he made slow, but consistent, progress toward the wreckage.

As he neared, heat prickled across his face like pokers of fire. His nerves tingled, fraying. It was a large van, seating twelve or fifteen, with room in the back for luggage. It had landed on its roof, melted tires oozing onto the wheels as they jutted up in the air. It smelled of spent fuel and char and as Clint stopped a foot away, the heat from the last of the fire warmed his face.

He swallowed, hard, and steeled himself. It was a miracle the rest of the forest didn't burn in the explosion, but thanks to the landslide, the van sat all alone on a river of dirt, stopped only by an outcropping of rock and a solitary pine tree, now a blackened toothpick pointing toward the sky.

He took a deep breath and ducked low enough to catch a glimpse inside. The sight stole his breath. Bodies, baked and burned beyond recognition sat, upside down in their seats, fused to the warped and melted seat cushions. Clint fumbled as he eased closer and reached out to grip the crumpled metal frame of the van. It was warm to the touch.

The wretched smell of burnt flesh and hair assaulted his nose and he staggered backward, retching. The contents of his stomach spilled out into the dirt: borrowed water and a protein bar. He wiped his mouth with the back of his hand.

He still didn't know if it was Mika's van. It could have been another trip, another set of kids setting out to enjoy the long weekend. He turned around, searching the ground for any cast off debris. If the landslide hit the van, then maybe there were packs or supplies scattered about.

Maybe he could eliminate the van as a possible death trap for his daughter.

Clint followed the path of destruction, casting his gaze about the dirt and rocks, moving broken branches and bushes aside as he climbed. Fifty feet up the mountain, no more than a handful of steps from where he'd climbed down, he spotted something. He reached down between dirt-coated leaves and pulled out a tattered paperback. He turned it over in his hands. The cover was missing, but the first page stilled him.

Written in bubbly handwriting was the name Sasha Williams. He sucked in a breath. Mika wasn't great friends with Sasha, but they'd been in the same Girl Scout troop for years. He turned around, cupped his hands around his mouth and shouted, "Mika! Mika!" His voice slashed through the trees, carried with the breeze. He screamed her name until his throat was raw, until his vocal cords were strained to their limit.

Maybe she'd made it out of the van. Maybe she wasn't roasted into a charcoal skeleton inside. He turned back to the ground, searching anew for any evidence. Any sign his daughter was either there or gone. A hint of something green and smooth peeked through a gap in the dirt and Clint dove for it, fingers clawing through the dirt and rubble to pull out a nylon green stuff sack.

He opened it and his heart nosedived into his stomach. He fell back on his heels, unable to keep his breathing steady. Inside the bag was a collection of cell phones, all with candy-colored cases. One by one, he pulled them out. An iPhone with a bubble gum pink case with a unicorn sticker. An android with a clear glitter case and a matching Pop Socket.

As his fingers wrapped around the next phone, he recoiled as if he'd been burned. His breath hitched, hand hovering an inch above the familiar lavender case. Devastation settled low and heavy in Clint's gut as he pulled out Mika's phone.

Tears blurred Clint's vision. Disbelief and anguish wrapped itself around Clint's heart, but he forced himself to stand. He called out again, even louder this time than last, "Mika! Mika!"

He combed the area. Perhaps she was too weak, or too injured to call out for him. Maybe she'd been thrown from the van or escaped before it fell. Maybe she'd gotten out and decided to walk, something in her gut telling her to leave the vehicle. He kept searching, working his way out from the wreckage in a spiral all while calling her name over and over.

When he reached a flat area where the landslide tapered off and undisturbed forest began, he sagged to his knees. Sweat covered his brow, dripped from his nose, soaked his hair. Clint had to accept the truth. If Mika were still alive, she'd never have left her phone behind. She'd never have given up and wandered down the mountain without it. He'd drilled it into her to contact him at the first sign of trouble. That's what she would have done.

Not run down the mountain and into the woods. Not left the scene of the accident all on her own. He stared up at the burned out shell of the van. A guttural sob rose in his throat as he exhaled his heavy grief and despair. His shoulders shook. Agony consumed him. Sagging to the ground, he crumpled like a balled up piece of paper into the dirt, hands clutched over his head to block out reality. He wailed Mika's name.

He had been so sure he would find her alive. So sure he was on a rescue mission. But the van, and the bodies, and bag of cell phones... The last of his hope fell to the dirt with his tears, mixing into mud. Her name rose from his throat in a tortured wail. His daughter was gone. He'd failed her.

CHAPTER TWENTY-SEVEN
MIKA

Mika froze, foot hovering an inch above the ground. *It couldn't be.* She tilted her head, listening to the rustle of leaves. She swore she'd heard a voice, a shout. Something like her name on the wind.

But everyone who knew her name, everyone who'd been with her on this fated trip, was gone. She shook her head to clear it and kept walking. Where, she wasn't sure exactly. But at some point, she'd left the undisturbed forest and the trail she'd stumbled open behind and once again entered a landslide-ravaged area.

She had no way of knowing whether she'd circled back toward the burned-out van and the hope of a nearby road, or if she'd gone in the complete opposite direction, finding another landslide all together. But at least she was moving. If she kept heading down the slope, at some point she would reach either civilization or a campsite. At least she hoped so.

The wind picked up, this time carrying the same voice, but louder, more distinct. "Mika!"

Her hand flew to her mouth. It wasn't her mind playing tricks on her or her hope mutating some bird's squawk into her name. It was her father. Calling to her.

"Dad! Dad! Over here!" She yelled as loud as she could, raising up on her tip toes as if the extra two inches would make all the difference. "Dad!"

She waited, out of breath, cheeks reddened from effort. No reply. It was him, she was sure of it. Mika twisted around, eyes darting from tree to rock to wave of dirt. Where was he? Where did his voice come from? She closed her eyes and thought it over, struggling to pluck the direction from her memory.

From the left, somewhere above her. She opened her eyes and took off, beating back the branches and the dirt and the wayward debris as she called out, "Dad! Dad, can you hear me?"

As she climbed, her breathing grew labored and heavy. Her pulse rocketing through her ears muffled the world and ruined any chance of hearing her father. After a few hundred feet, she paused, hand on her hip as she sucked in a lungful of air. She hadn't imagined it, wasn't going crazy. He was out there.

She step off again, this time slower and more controlled, still working her way up in elevation, but not so quickly. She could still listen, still strain to hear his voice.

As she neared a massive, uprooted tree, the wind

shifted and once again his voice called out, only this time it wasn't to her. It was... about her. Full of hurt and anguish. Mika called to him and broke into a near-run, skirting the roots stretching twenty feet in either direction.

Hold on, Dad. I'm here. I'm coming.

With one hand digging into the dirty roots to gain leverage, Mika hauled herself over the fallen tree and into an area devastated by the landslide. She blinked in shock. There, in the dirt, was her father. Only she'd never seen him so... broken.

He hovered above the ground, half-hunched, half-curled around a bag. The sun reflected off the wetness streaking his cheeks. He was crying. Mika had never seen her father cry.

She called to him, hands waving frantically in the air as she closed the distance. He lifted his head, confusion furrowing his brow and tipping his lips into a frown. But it didn't matter. She barreled into him, arms out wide, and wrapped him in a hug as they both fell to the ground in a heap.

"Dad! Dad, you found me!" She squeezed so tight, her arms ached from the effort. "You really found me."

"Mika?" Her father struggled to upright them both. He reached for her shoulders and pushed her back, holding her an arm's length away as he stared, slack jawed at her face. It took a moment for reality to catch up to her father. His face transformed in slow motion from a frown to a smile so wide it split his lower lip. He crushed her to him, giant arms enveloping her in a dirty, sweat-soaked embrace.

"Mika! You're alive!" He pulled back. "When I found the van and the phones..."

She wiped back a sudden onslaught of tears. "The van crashed in the quake. I think... I think we were hit by the landslide. I was thrown to the floor and blacked out."

Her father shook his head in disbelief. "I thought you were still in there."

Mika swallowed. "Almost everyone died. Only Hampton and I survived the crash."

Her father glanced around. "Where is she? Is she hurt? Does she need help?"

Pain and loss welled up in Mika's throat and she couldn't hold it back. Tears streamed down her face and she tried to explain, but all that came out were jagged sobs.

He pulled her back into his warm embrace. "Shh. It's okay." His hand stroked her hair and after a few minutes she managed to explain all she'd been through.

It came out in bursts, accentuated by fits of crying and coughing, but at last, she finished. "I was completely turned around. I just knew I needed to head down the slope, and hoped that would be enough. I didn't know I was so close to the van. So close to..." She broke off, unable to speak anymore.

Her father shifted until she leaned against his chest and they stayed like that, him holding her up as she cried, until the tears dried on her cheeks and she felt some semblance of calm. "I'm proud of you, honey."

The words seeped deep into Mika's heart and lingered, filling a bit of the empty hole. "I should have saved Hampton. Should have stayed awake, kept her alive."

"It sounds like she had internal bleeding, honey, probably on the brain. That's what happened to Charlie, you remember him? The guy at work who rode the motorcycle?"

Mika nodded against her father's chest.

"He was in that accident and refused to go to the hospital, said he was fine. That night he was talking gibberish to his girlfriend, not making any sense. He went to sleep and never woke up. Autopsy showed a massive brain bleed from the crash impact."

She stared at her hands. "So even if I got her off the mountain..."

"Hampton would have died without surgery. And most of the hospitals are gone."

Mika sucked in a breath. "The quake was that strong?"

"Mika—"

Her father paused and she glanced up at him, reading the trepidation on his face. "What is it?"

He pressed his lips together, stared off into the distance for a moment. "Port Angeles is ruined. Hospitals, the Port... We probably don't have a house anymore."

She blinked. "Was the quake that bad?"

"It wasn't the quake. It was the tsunami."

"What?" Mika reeled. "What tsunami?"

"It hit Port Angeles about a half hour after the quake subsided, a massive wall of water coming in from the

Strait. Half the town was ripped out to sea, the ground disintegrated. The rest is flooded. People are taking shelter in the elementary school."

Mika glanced around them. She'd thought the landslide was the worst of their issues. But a massive flood? Her eyes widened as she turned back to her dad. "What about Mom? She's in Bellevue. Did it flood? What about Seattle?"

His gaze skated away.

"Dad, come on." She tugged on his sleeve. "Tell me."

"Based on the flooding in Port Angeles, hon, I'm guessing Seattle is gone. And Bellevue... There can't be much left."

She took her dad's hand and squeezed it, waited until he looked her in the eyes. "Dad, we have to find her. We have to find Mom."

When he didn't reply, a fresh wave of tears threatened to coat her lashes, but she blinked them away, jaw locked with iron determination.

"Mika—" Her father stood slowly and ran a hand over his face. He looked down at her with that look he had whenever he was about to let her down easy, whenever she was about to be disappointed.

She wouldn't let him start. "No." She struggled to her feet. "No, we're not going to assume Mom didn't make it. As soon as we get off this mountain, we check on the house, see whether there's anything to salvage and head to Bellevue. We have to find her, Dad. We have to."

"You don't understand." The shadows under her father's eyes looked like half-moon bruises, dark purple, almost black. "The chances of finding your mother..." he trailed off. A deep set wrinkle bridged his eyebrows. "There's going to be all sorts of rescue and recovery people on the ground. FEMA, National Guard. They probably won't even let us in."

Mika's stomach catapulted into her throat and she balled her fists at her sides. They weren't going to abandon her to a bunch of strangers. Even if she'd left them. Even if she'd chosen those strangers over her family. Mika's nose burned as new tears came and her throat ached as snot slid down it. "Can't we at least try?"

Her father released a heavy sigh and rubbed the creases from his forehead with the tips of his fingers.

"If she *is* alive, she needs us," Mika pressed.

"Mika, she might already be—you know..." Agony crinkled the skin around her father's eyes.

Mika reached out and clamped a hand on her father's arm. "You came for me, and I was alive. What if *she* is too, and no one is there to find her? To help her? What if she's trapped somewhere, waiting for help that never comes?"

Her father tilted his head to the sky, staring past her at something more than clouds.

"Alright." The single word filled Mika with hope. "We'll give it a shot. We'll go until we hit a dead end." He paused, gave his daughter a steadfast look. "But I'm not putting you in danger. Not after all we've been through. I can't risk losing you again."

Mika nodded and clutched her father around his solid frame, hugging him close. "We can't give up on her, Dad. We just can't."

Clint and Mika hiked out of the forest devastated by landslides and found the truck as the sun slipped behind the still-standing trees. As they piled into the vehicle, Clint stole a glance at his daughter, something he'd been doing every few minutes since he'd found her. It was a miracle, truly.

His heart went out to the families of the other girls and the troop leaders, but Mika was alive. She'd found a way to survive through what sounded like tremendous odds. First the landslide, then the rollover, then Hampton growing ill and dying. He shook his head as he cranked the engine.

"What?"

He glanced at Mika. "Just amazed at how strong you are. You're a fighter, hon."

Mika glanced out the passenger side window, saying nothing. Survivor's guilt ate away at her, that much was obvious. But it wasn't her fault the others died. In time, she would understand.

It was slow going, making their way back through the debris toward Port Angeles. In the time it had taken Clint to find his daughter, another section of mountain had given way, rock and dirt cascading across the road and blocking their path. He backtracked, but was unable to find another way through. Forced to off-road, Clint eased his way through brush and rocks, around trees and landslide debris, until he found a road running parallel to Port Angeles. It was the long way around, but eventually, they should make it home.

Or what was left of home, anyway.

Mika stayed quiet and Clint's thoughts drifted to Daphne. Mika's conviction, her steadfast determination to find her mother, worried Clint. Daphne lived in Bellevue. If it wasn't leveled to the ground, it was flooded, for sure. The chance Daphne survived such an onslaught was slim. The woman was resourceful, sure, but she wasn't experienced in situations like this. Roughing it. Surviving.

When the going got tough...

Daphne left. Clint shoved his anger down. He still loved his wife. Always would. But it was hard to keep the resentment at bay. Hard to deal with her choice to leave instead of work it out. Maybe he'd been distant in those last few months. Focused on his job and Mika and not so much his wife at home. But she hadn't volunteered either.

There was so much he would say to her if she were

still alive. So many things they'd left unsaid. But doubted he would ever have the chance. Daphne was most likely gone. Mika would have to deal with the loss of her mother and the loss of her friends.

He tightened his grip on the steering wheel and sat taller in the seat as he shoved his spiraling thoughts aside and focused on the road. They found a road running north-south and finally turned toward Port Angeles. As they eased out of the tree line of the National Park, the faint glow of an electric light caught Clint's eye. He slowed.

To their west, the sunset painted the sky smoky orange and gray. To their east, a small building sat on the corner, a single light on outside. Mika rolled down her window. "What is that sound?"

Clint strained to listen. "Generator, I think." He motioned at the building. "What is that place?"

Mika leaned forward. "I think it's a restaurant." She squinted into the fading light. "Duke's Foothill Diner." She turned with excitement. "They might have something to eat."

Clint cast a doubtful look at the place. "It's been a while without power. Can't imagine anything they have is still good."

"Dad. I'm starving. You've got to be, too. The light's on outside and the door is open. We should check it out."

Clint pulled into the vacant parking lot. Any other time, he'd have passed this hole-in-the-wall and never given it a second glance. But his stomach rumbled as he reached for the door handle. Any food was better than no food at this point. He glanced at Mika. "You stay behind me. In case there's trouble."

She screwed up her face. "Trouble from what?"

He didn't answer, just waited until she rolled her eyes and agreed to walk behind him. Clint pulled the screen door open and a bell signaled their arrival. A lone man leaned on the counter, white apron covering his front. He reached over to a small portable TV and turned the sound down as they approached. "Evening."

"Are you open by any chance?"

The man smiled. "Sure are. But menu's limited. Everything in the freezer's gone bad and I can't run the fryer off the generator."

Clint nodded and eased onto a cracked vinyl barstool opposite the man. Mika did the same. He looked the man over. Mid-50s, balding, shirt stretched tight across his belly. A tired and worn nameplate pinned to his chest read *Don*. "You the owner?"

"Yep. Been here goin' on twenty-five years. You a ranger?"

Clint shook his head. "Work at the Port down in town."

The man whistled. "From the TV coverage, not much left of Port Angeles."

"I'm aware." Clint glanced at his daughter. "So what's on the menu?"

Don patted his stomach. "I've got ham and turkey sandwiches, potato chips, and half an apple berry crumb pie that's on its last legs."

Mika glanced at her father. "Can we have all of it?"

Don laughed and waited for Clint to nod. "A bit of everything, coming right up."

As he headed toward the back, Clint stopped him. "Mind if you turn the TV back up?"

Don reached out and turned the knob. "Afraid all the news is bad, but be my guest."

Clint propped his forearms on the counter and leaned closer. The screen, one of the old-school cathode-ray tube types, was barely ten inches across. Mika squeezed next to him to see. Together, they watched as a flooded out city shot from what he assumed was a drone, paraded across the screen.

Clint swallowed as he read the ticker:

CITY OF SEATTLE DESTROYED. FLOOD WATERS REFUSE TO RECEDE.

A reporter's voice cut in over the aerial footage

"Water levels remain high in much of Seattle and Bellevue, with multiple stories still underwater in the heart of the city. Estimates place the initial tidal surge at forty feet above sea level, a tsunami of unprecedented magnitude. Government officials from FEMA to the National Guard to the military are deployed along the coast, establishing emergency shelters and aiding in rescue and recovery efforts."

Clint pressed his lips together. It was as bad as he feared.

"Devastation runs from Vancouver to the California-Oregon border with hundreds of miles of coastline and millions of buildings underwater. Until the waters recede, which experts are saying could take anywhere from days to weeks, we won't know the full extent of the damage. Government officials are asking anyone in the inundation zone to evacuate immediately. FEMA has set up white receiving tents at the edge of the flooding providing emergency medical care and transport to their main shelter now established in Ellensburg."

Don's rounded shoulders blocked the TV as he set plates in front of Mika and Clint. A sandwich loaded with meat and cheese sat beside a heaping serving of potato chips. "When you're done with these, I'll have the pie ready. Coffee?"

Clint nodded in appreciation. "That would be great."

He dug into the food, ignoring the sour taste in the back of this throat still lingering from the broadcast. Beside him, Mika sniffed. He glanced at his daughter. Red rimmed her glassy eyes and she wiped beneath her nose with the back of her hand. There wasn't any way to sugar coat the scenes on the television. Any hope Mika had of finding her mother alive must be dashed now.

He rubbed her back for a moment. "You should eat."

She snuffed again and nodded before picking up a potato chip. It crunched in her mouth as she stared vacantly at the screen. Clint forced down another bite of sandwich, meat and cheese now as flavorful as cardboard.

"Dad!" Mika's finger jabbed toward the TV. "Look!"

He glanced at the screen. The drone hovered over what at first glance appeared to be one of countless streets in the business district of downtown Bellevue.

Mika grabbed his free hand and squeezed. "Isn't that mom's office? The one with the green roof?"

Clint squinted and leaned closer. "I don't know, Mika. There have to be tons of buildings just like it."

"No, Dad, look!" She let his hand go to point again. "There's the bank building two over, with the helicopter pad on top. Mom told me they put it in just for one fancy client. It's weird because it's got the bank logo on the pad - a diamond inside a circle."

He wasn't convinced. "That could be anywhere."

"It's not." Mika's tone bordered on anger. She stared at the screen as the reporter spoke again.

"We're now showing footage of Bellevue Way where many buildings suffered catastrophic damage but a few remain standing. Water in this area has begun to recede, although not as quickly as officials had hoped. Check back at our eleven o'clock broadcast when we'll have a reporter on the ground."

"Now do you believe me?"

Clint exhaled. Mika was right. That was the area of Daphne's office building. If the green-roofed building really was hers, then she might have survived. She might still be there, hunkered down, waiting for rescue.

He thought about all the obstacles between them and Bellevue: broken roads, landslides, floodwater. Desperate people. None of it mattered if the mother of his child was alive, waiting. Clint squeezed his daughter's hand. "If she's out there, sweetheart, I promise you, we'll find a way to reach her."

————

Thank you for reading *Fault Lines: Upheaval*. Subscribe to Harley's newsletter to be notified when book two in the series is released.

www.harleytate.com/subscribe

———

In the meantime, if you are new to Harley's work and are interested in more, check out the *After the EMP* series:

If the power grid fails, how far will you go to survive?

Madison spends her days tending plants as an agriculture student at the University of California, Davis. She plans to graduate and put those skills to work only a few hours from home in the Central Valley. The sun has always been her friend, until now.

When catastrophe strikes, how prepared will you be?

Tracy starts her morning like any other, kissing her husband Walter goodbye before heading off to work at the local public library. She never expects it to end fleeing for her life in a Suburban full of food and water. Tackling life's daily struggles is one thing, preparing to survive when it all crashes down is another.

The end of the world brings out the best and worst in all of us.

With no communication and no word from the government, the Sloanes find themselves grappling with the end of the modern world all on their own. Will Madison and her friends have what it takes to make it back to Sacramento and her family? Can Tracy fend off looters and thieves and help her friends and neighbors survive?

The EMP is only the beginning.

———

ALSO BY HARLEY TATE

FALLING SKIES

Fire and Ashes

Thunder and Acid

Wind and Chaos

Escape and Evade

War and Survival

———

AFTER THE EMP

Darkness Falls (exclusive newsletter prequel)

Darkness Begins

Darkness Grows

Darkness Rises

Chaos Comes

Chaos Gains

Chaos Evolves

Hope Sparks

Hope Stumbles

Hope Survives

NUCLEAR SURVIVAL

First Strike (exclusive newsletter prequel)

Southern Grit:

Brace for Impact

Escape the Fall

Survive the Panic

Northern Exposure:

Take the Hit

Duck for Cover

Ride it Out

Western Strength:

Bear the Brunt

Shelter in Place

Make the Cut

NO ORDINARY DAY

No Ordinary Escape

No Ordinary Day

No Ordinary Getaway

No Ordinary Mission

Find all of Harley's releases on Amazon today: www.amazon.
com/author/harleytate.

ACKNOWLEDGMENTS

Thank you for reading book one in the *Fault Lines* series.

As I've mentioned before, a few liberties have been taken, especially with place names and other minor details in writing this novel. I hope you don't hold it against me!

If you enjoyed this book and have a moment, please consider leaving a review on Amazon. Every one helps new readers discover my work and helps me keep writing the stories you want to read.

Until next time,

Harley

When the world as we know it falls apart, how far will you go to survive?

Harley Tate writes edge-of-your-seat post-apocalyptic fiction exploring what happens when ordinary people are faced with impossible choices.

The apocalypse is only the beginning.

Find out more at:
www.harleytate.com

Made in United States
Troutdale, OR
09/22/2023

13097787R00145